Rooster

Don Trembath

ORCA BOOK PUBLISHERS

National Library of Canada Cataloguing in Publication Data

Trembath, Don, 1963-
Rooster / Don Trembath.

ISBN 1-55143-261-7

I. Title.

PS8589.R392R66 2005   jC813'.54   C2005-901966-2

Summary: Rooster wants to graduate from high school,
he just doesn't want to work for it.

First published in the United States, 2005
Library of Congress Control Number: 2005924421

Orca Book Publishers gratefully acknowledges the support for its publishing
programs provided by the following agencies: the Government of Canada
through the Book Publishing Industry Development Program (BPIDP), the
Canada Council for the Arts, and the British Columbia Arts Council.

Cover design and typesetting: Lynn O'Rourke
Cover photography: Getty Images

Orca Book Publishers   Orca Book Publishers
Box 5626, Stn. B   PO Box 468
Victoria, BC Canada   Custer, WA USA
V8R 6S4   98240-0468

Printed and bound in Canada
08 07 06 05 • 5 4 3 2 1

To my mom,
small in stature, big in support,
encouragement, laughter,
companionship, character and love.

1

Gloria Nixon was furious with the way things had gone, but as she well knew, how she felt about things didn't matter. Not at Winston High School, anyway. No way. At Winston High School, if you weren't the school principal and your name wasn't Judith Helmsley, what you thought or cared about or said meant nothing. Gloria knew it, and everyone else knew it too.

That didn't matter either, of course. How Gloria felt and what she knew fell into the same category. But, dammit, she was irritated! Especially this time. As a matter of fact, this time she was so irritated, so frustrated and so annoyed, she came *this* close to saying something. *This* close!

"I was ready to let her have it," she told her husband, Bernie, at lunch. She was talking to him on her cell phone from the front seat of her car. Her hands were still shaking as she talked, and her head hurt from the stress of it all, which was not a good sign. Slim, neat, extremely health-conscious and meticulously well-groomed, Gloria was nevertheless vulnerable to headaches that could sideline her for days and rashes that would haunt her for weeks when anxiety got the better of her.

"Good for you," said Bernie, himself an elementary school teacher on the opposite side of town. Gloria had become one of the three guidance counselors at Winston High last year. They were both twenty-seven. They'd been teaching for four years and married for two.

"She thinks she can push anyone around." Gloria's nostrils flared as she spoke.

"She obviously doesn't know you very well."

"Next time she does something like this, that's it."

"Now you're talking."

"I'm going to tell her to take this job and shove it."

"Careful now. We've got eight years left on the mortgage, and that car you're sitting in isn't paid for either."

Ironically, as Gloria sat in her brand-new, candy-apple-red, freshly washed and waxed BMW, the very student she was most upset with walked past her. Roy Cobb, or Rooster, as he was better known, was a tall thin kid with dark spiky hair and a pointed nose. He had two earrings in his right ear and another on his right nipple, which he insisted on showing off whenever the weather allowed for it by taking off his shirt and strutting around the school grounds. He was smoking, as usual, although God only knew what. Gloria shook her head and followed him with her eyes.

The file on Rooster was as thick as any she had in her office: His father died when he was ten. His mother, Eunice, thin and pointy as well, and a pain, if the truth be known, remarried three years ago. Irving was her new husband. He was a former baseball player, apparently. None of the gym teachers had ever heard of him.

Rooster had no brothers or sisters, a fact that provided Gloria with the only sense of relief she ever felt when discussing him with her colleagues, or even just thinking about him, as she was now. He was born and raised right here in the small city of Winston, Alberta, population 47,000. He was in grade twelve at Winston High.

Gloria had been his English teacher in grade ten. At the start of that school year, she'd made the mistake of announcing to her students that she'd gotten married over the summer. From that day on, Rooster announced her arrival in the classroom each morning with a noisy rendition of "Here Comes the Bride." He oohed over her engagement ring but wondered aloud why it wasn't a bit bigger. "Did he get you something else with it?

An Xbox or a stereo or something?" He continually referred to her husband as her "old man," and when, in an uncharacteristically public display of anger, she told him that the next time he called Bernie an old man, she'd bring Bernie to school to talk to Rooster personally, Rooster switched to calling him her "kept man" and began wondering aloud what other sorts of things she let him do.

Her frustration mounted with each writing assignment he submitted. Generally regarded as a lazy student who wasted his potential at every turn, there was no questioning his ability as a writer—when he chose to put his mind to it.

The closet in my mother's bedroom is a cluttered jumble of shoes, pantsuits, bright summer dresses and very small bras, he penned for his assignment on descriptive writing. *She hides chocolate bars and hard candies on the top shelf, a habit from when I was small and constantly hounding her for something fun to eat. On the floor in the back right corner is a box of old photographs, including many of my father, who is dead now. She still cries occasionally when she looks at them, which is why there is always a box of Kleenex nearby, and little balls of used tissues on the floor.*

"He writes better than some of my best students," she would moan in the staff room. "He doesn't even have to try."

In grade eleven, he began asking her if there were any "little Bernies" on the way yet. When she scolded him one day for asking about things that were "extremely personal," Rooster said, "Wow, I figured old Bernie would be too young to have problems like that."

By grade twelve, he'd found an additional target for his troublesome ways in the form of Mr. Taylor, a kind, passive English teacher who fervently believed that kids must find their own passions in order to pursue them with the vigor necessary to learn. "I want you to write a book report on any book you choose," he said, with a level of joy that no one in the class could quite understand. "I'm not going to burden you with one of my choices. I want *you* to choose. Anything. Anything at all."

Rooster selected *Penthouse Forum: The Anthology*, 2003 edition. The essay he wrote was entitled, *"Penthouse:* Great reading, but where's the love?"

Sure, I have a greater appreciation for co-ed aerobics classes, and who knew working overtime could be so enjoyable? But you do get tired of it all after a while, don't you? I mean, I didn't, but not all adults are like the people in this book, are they?

Mr. Taylor had not anticipated this response to his assignment.

"Can we do a pictorial essay on the same topic next time?" Rooster asked when the written essays were finished.

"That would not be appropriate," said Mr. Taylor, blushing slightly.

"Speak for yourself," said Rooster.

Gloria shuddered to think of what might be coming next from the boy. And while she was happy to know that he would be leaving the school for good in a few months—if his marks permitted him to graduate, that is—she had spent more than a few minutes wondering what was in store for him in the future.

"Why waste your time?" Bernie had said to her just last week. "He'll be out of your hair soon. That's a good thing."

"He's still a young person graduating from *my* school who will be living in *my* town," said Gloria earnestly. "I think it's natural to think about."

"You think he might do something to the house?" said Bernie, suddenly frowning.

"Or the car. He has no scruples. He's proven that already."

Rooster's dismal history made the decision earlier in the day by Principal Helmsley to involve him in Gloria's plan to get students more active in the community almost impossible to comprehend.

"Who?" Gloria had said in their meeting, her brain refusing to accept what her ears had unmistakably heard.

"Rooster Cobb. He's perfect for it. Talk to him after school. We have to get moving on this. The year's almost over."

In fact, Gloria's plan had been to partner some of the "star" students at Winston High with places like Common House in the same way that other kids sign up for work experience programs, except the emphasis would be on volunteerism, and social and community awareness.

"We'll go the star-student route next year," Principal Helmsley said, leaning back in her chair. She was a big, intimidating woman, standing over six feet tall on size twelve feet. She could palm a volleyball without effort and was known to patrol the hallways at school like a drill sergeant examining the troops. Her white hair was short and severe, much like her sense of humor. She wore glasses that magnified the heat that came from her eyes when she was angry. "For now, Rooster's your boy."

"May I ask why?"

Principal Helmsley came forward in her chair. "This is it for him. His last chance. He does well, we can see about getting him out of here at graduation. If he blows it, too bad. He's back again in the fall for another year, or he can live his life as a high-school dropout. See how far that gets him."

In hindsight, this was the point in the conversation where Gloria had felt that she had enough anger and courage inside her to speak out against Principal Helmsley's idea. This was the exact moment that she was referring to when she had talked to Bernie.

"But that's not the point of all this!" she had wanted to say. "This is to reward the special people in our community, and to give the best of our students the opportunity to show the world how truly great they really are. This is so the young people and the old people and the special needs people can come together and *share* and *grow* and do *beautiful* things with each other. You're turning it into a final testing ground for a worthless little twerp who we already know is going to fail miserably and take the school's honor with him and probably crush the spirits of the people he's working with. I think that's wrong! I think you're wrong, Mrs. Helmsley! You are absolutely, totally dead wrong, *and I am not going to stand for it*!!"

Instead, Gloria had said nothing. She accepted Principal Helmsley's revisions without comment or complaint and returned to her office to make the required phone calls, beginning first with Common House, the town of Winston's home for adults with special needs, both physical and mental, where her proposal was enthusiastically accepted.

"We've had so many budget cuts here lately," the program coordinator, a woman named Pam Yuler, said. "We'll take anyone you can give us."

"That's about who you'll get," said Gloria, not intending to be smart, but feeling no guilt for saying it.

"Why don't we start him or her in the Games Room? We hold spelling bees there. We play musical chairs. Indoor golf."

"It'll be a he. Do you have anything else?" Gloria could not see Rooster in a Games Room filled with people who were either physically unable to help themselves, or mentally incapable of much more than reading a children's book or spelling their own names, if that.

There was a pause as Mrs. Yuler thought for a moment. "Let me talk to the floor staff. They're a bit more in touch with some of these things than I am. Can I have your number?"

Gloria had given her the number on her cell phone as well as in her office. She knew she'd be spending some time in her car over lunch. The car was her refuge during stressful times like this: a safe place to which she could go for comfort, peace and the intoxicating smell of new leather.

She closed her eyes to ease the strain on her head, then opened them with a start when something banged against her windshield. It was Rooster, his face pressed tight against the glass, smiling at her with the wide-eyed delirium of a homicidal maniac.

Gloria suppressed the urge to scream and rolled down her window.

"Scared you, didn't I?" Rooster beamed with delight. At least his friends weren't with him, she thought. That would have made a bad situation even worse.

"Yes, you did, a little. What can I do for you, Rooster?" Gloria's heart rate slowly began to settle. "Get your hands off the car, please. I just had it waxed."

"You can tell," said Rooster, running his fingers along the side panels. "She's smooth."

"What do you want, Rooster?"

"That's what I'm here to ask you. Mrs. Jarvis in the office said you wanted to see me about something. I remembered seeing you out here daydreaming in your car, so I thought I'd come back and check."

Gloria sighed and briefly shook her head. "I wasn't daydreaming. I was relaxing and recharging."

"Oh yeah?"

"Yeah."

"I like that. I'll have to remember that for math tomorrow. 'Honest, Mr. Armstrong. I wasn't daydreaming. I was relaxing and recharging.'"

"You should try to stay awake in math tomorrow. You have a test, as I recall."

Rooster grimaced as he remembered the test. Then he changed the subject. "So, what did you want me for?"

Gloria had to think for a moment before she could explain. In truth, *she* did not want to see him for anything ever again. It was Sergeant Helmsley who wanted her to see him, and for reasons that Gloria still could not fully understand.

"Can we talk about this tomorrow? How about first thing? Nine o'clock in my office."

"How about now? I have to study first thing. I have a math test, remember?" Rooster pulled a package of cigarettes from his coat pocket and tapped out a fresh smoke.

"You should study for that tonight."

The ringing of Gloria's cell phone put a temporary stop to their conversation. It was Mrs. Yuler from

Common House. She'd talked to some of the other staff members and they had given her a few more ideas. The kitchen could always use an extra hand, the laundry crew was overwhelmed and the bowling team still needed a supervisor.

"Excuse me?" said Gloria, shooing Rooster and his cigarette smoke away from her car. She cupped her hand over the receiver and hissed at him, "Tomorrow at nine. My office." Then she returned to Mrs. Yuler. "I didn't hear that last one. What was it again? A bowling team?"

"It's not really a team. We have four people here who like to go bowling. It was their own idea a few years ago. One of them used to bowl quite a bit and she got a few of the others involved. So twice a week we'd put them on the Common House bus and take them down to the bowling alley here in town and they'd have a great time. But we had to stop that with all the cuts we've had this year."

"What does the supervisor do?"

"Well, he would meet the team down at the alley and see that they all got back. Make sure everyone's okay."

Gloria thought for a moment.

"That was the job that most of the girls here wanted filled, actually," Mrs. Yuler said. "They said it would take care of a lot of the trouble they've been having if the Strikers could get back on their feet again."

"The Strikers?"

"That's what they call themselves. They like to think of themselves as a team."

Gloria watched Rooster as he drifted across the parking lot, away from the school.

"What kind of trouble could they cause?"

"Oh, the Strikers are a very interesting group. Two of them are extremely loud, some would say obnoxious, which I would tend to agree with, but that's just me. The third one never seems to stop talking, which can get on your nerves, although he's much cheerier than the first two, and the fourth one, Dorothy-Jane-Anne, is the quiet one. She doesn't say much, but she usually creates more chaos than the rest of them put together. And lately, because they haven't been bowling at all, they've been letting their frustrations get the better of them, and it's been causing some problems."

"Really." Rooster was no longer in sight.

"Oh, yes. They're quite a bunch. They'd be a challenge for anyone. A real challenge."

A small smile began to creep across Gloria's lips. Could this be what Mrs. Helmsley was thinking when she revised Gloria's plan?

"I understand you have a real challenge at your end to find a task for."

"Yes, yes, we do," said Gloria, still smiling. Then, quickly, she frowned. "How did you know that?"

"I spoke with Judith."

"You know Judith Helmsley?"

"We play bridge together. I called her this afternoon, just before I called you. It's our bridge night tonight. I had to know if she was coming or not."

"Did she know about the Strikers?"

"I assume so. I don't know for sure. I know her daughter's been a volunteer here for some time now, so she probably knows something about them."

"No kidding."

"Oh, yes. Elma's been here every Sunday afternoon for three or four years. So, I don't know what Judith knows or doesn't know. It's a good idea, though. We could sure use the help, providing he comes."

"Oh, he will," said Gloria, with renewed confidence. "We'll be by tomorrow after school. They'll want to meet him first, I'm sure, before they get to work."

"They'll interview him. That's what they do whenever someone new comes along. They'll sit him down and they'll interview him. I've seen them do it before. It's very entertaining. I hope he makes it through."

Gloria was beaming when she snapped shut her cell phone. She stepped out of her car with a smile on her face and shut the door. She saw the smudges from Rooster's fingertips all over the side panels and around the front to the hood. She didn't care.

Suddenly she was not upset at all.

2

*A*fter leaving Mrs. Nixon, Rooster went for a walk through the ravine. It was his favorite place in Winston. The city had paved the pathway that ran through the trees and along the Winston River three years ago, making it a perfect place for cyclists, skaters, joggers and walkers alike to do their thing.

Rooster took one last pull on his cigarette and flicked the butt into a muddy puddle. He exhaled the smoke through his nose and buried his hands in his jacket pockets.

It was one o'clock and he had nothing to do. That wasn't exactly true. He had school to do, but school had become even more difficult than usual to get up for in recent weeks. The thought of attending classes every day was almost as hard to take as the reality that very soon his days as a student in the Winston public school system would be over.

Rooster himself was only vaguely aware of his predicament. To him, school was the same in grade twelve as it had been since the beginning of junior high: boring, irrelevant, a place to go to get out of the house.

He wrote about these feelings once in a grade eleven essay. The topic had been "If you could change one thing in the world, what would it be?"

Given that there would be quite a rush among my classmates to end world hunger, stop all wars and provide housing for the homeless, I think I'd tackle a smaller, yet still significant, issue—make schooling mandatory up to grade seven. After that, you're on your own.

People like Mrs. Nixon and Mr. Taylor made going to class slightly more tolerable only because they were so easy to tease and so entertaining when they became upset.

Especially Mrs. Nixon. Where they got her from was something he would like to know. She clipped around the hallways in her high heels every day, smiling and saying hi to kids who flipped her the bird as soon as her back was turned. At least Rooster said things to her face.

Principal Helmsley was at the other end of the scale from Mrs. Nixon. She was a monster. No kid in his right mind flipped her the bird, no matter which way her back was turned, because everyone knew she had eyes all around her head.

She also had a daughter, Elma. Rooster and his friends called Elma "Junior" because she was so much like her mother. Elma didn't like that.

"Don't call me Junior," she would say, her voice booming down the hallway exactly the way her mother's did. "I'm my own person."

"Okay, Junior," Rooster said the last time she hollared at them. "We won't call you Junior anymore, Junior."

Also like her mother, Elma was tough.

One day in gym, during a game of murder ball, she gave Andy Gilmore a bloody nose when she hit him flat in the face with the ball.

"I said nothing above the waist," cried Mr. Johnston, the gym teacher, holding a towel to Andy's nose.

"He ducked right into it," said Elma. She was holding a new ball in her hand, looking like she was ready to throw it at someone else.

"He did not duck. He didn't even see it coming."

"Then he should have ducked."

Mr. Johnston folded the towel so the bloody part was on the inside. "You do that again, you'll go right down to the office."

"If I do that again, he won't have a face left," Elma countered. "And I will if he opens his mouth one more time."

Aside from his girlfriend, Jolene, Rooster had two very good friends, both of whom he had known since childhood—Dennis Davis, better known as Puffs because of his gigantic puffy hair, and Jayson Cullen, the super-jock of Winston High.

Puffs was a little guy, built like a pillow, with soft stubby arms and legs sticking out. His parents, Mr. and Mrs. Puffs, as Rooster called them, were extremely rich and divorced. His father ran his own software business. His mom was a special events organizer. Puffs did work for both of them. He was a computer genius. Last year, with the help of his dad, he set up his own small business, Puffs On Tap, that provided quick, affordable help for the computer-challenged. It quickly made him a ton of money, most of which he invested, also with the help of his dad.

"My dad told me if I keep this up, I'll be a millionaire by the time I'm thirty," he told Rooster one day on their way to school.

"Why thirty?" said Rooster, who had never had such predictions come his way. "Why not twenty-seven, or thirty-two?"

"Good question. I'll have to ask him."

Puffs' other passion in life, apart from money and computers, was Gracie Armstrong, a classmate who had thick, wavy brown hair, long shapely legs, a beautiful shiny smile and a twenty-year-old boyfriend named Nick, who picked her up in his convertible every day after school. In the summer, when the sun was out, they drove around Winston with the top down, Gracie's hair flying in the wind like streamers trailing behind a kite.

Jolene hated Gracie and was constantly on Puffs' case about her. "What do you even see in her?"

"Isn't it obvious?"

"She's obnoxious. She's a big mouth in a body that will be smothered in fat by the time she's forty."

"That gives me twenty-three years."

"I bet she can't even read," said Jolene another time.

"And?" said Puffs. "Your point is?"

Jayson was a star in volleyball, basketball, track and rugby. After he graduated, he had full scholarship offers at universities across the country, including one for football from McGill University in Montreal, even though he hadn't played football for two years.

"Jayson doesn't know what he's gonna do yet," said Jayson the last time the topic of his future came up. At six feet, 190 pounds, with a shaved head and a tattoo of a scorpion on his right shoulder, Jayson looked the part of a jock. He also talked like one, in third person. "Jayson's not even sure he wants to go to school next year. He might wanna stay home and make some coin working for his dad."

Jayson's father owned a successful construction company.

"Maybe Jayson should stop calling himself Jayson before someone puts Jayson in a home," said Puffs one day.

"No one's gonna put Jayson in a home," said Jayson.

"Puffs will," said Puffs. "Puffs will build a big home for Jayson so Jayson can run around all day by himself, talking with all his friends named Jayson."

At the start of the school year, as a joke, Rooster put his writing talents to work and began sending Jayson love letters typed on an old typewriter that he had found during an outing with his mom to a thrift store. The first few were sent anonymously, but then he and Puffs came up with a better idea: he would give Jayson one letter at a time of the name of the person who was supposedly writing the letters. The next one he sent said, *Hey fella, I loved that move you put on that guy in the rugby game last weekend. I hope you save a few of those tricks for me. L.*

The name Rooster was spelling was Lavender. "It's the perfect stripper's name," he told Puffs. "Just what we're after." He got as far as Lav before Jayson said anything.

"Hey, Rooster," he said discreetly one day after school, before basketball practice. "Is Lav a name?"

"Lav?"

"Yeah."

Rooster took a moment to think about it. "I don't think so. Unless it's short for something, like lavatory. As in bathroom. Why?"

"No reason."

"You know someone who goes to the bathroom a lot? Maybe it's a nickname."

A week later, Rooster had added two more letters.

Hey Jayson, wouldn't that scorpion on your shoulder like a playmate? I have tattoos too, you know. Laven.

"Laven?" said Puffs, after Jayson stopped him in the hallway. "Sure, Laven's a name."

"It is?"

"It's the lead actor's name in that TV show, *The Gay Prince.* Laven McDonahue. Why?"

"There's no TV show called *The Gay Prince.*"

"Sure there is. It's on Bravo! the no-sports network. That's why you've never heard of it."

"*The Gay Prince?*"

"It's a good show from what I hear, if you're gay."

Finally, after Jayson had received two letters with the entire name Lavender spelled out for him, he told Puffs and Rooster what was going on.

"Holy crap," said Puffs. "That's awesome. You're getting love letters from some woman you don't even know. She's, like, a secret admirer."

"How do you know it's not just a girl?" said Jayson. "Like some kid our age who goes to a different school."

"Come on, buddy." Puffs gave Jayson a knock on the shoulder. "Nobody names their kid Lavender. Lavender's a name you change your old name into after you become an exotic dancer."

"He's right," said Rooster. "A name like Joan doesn't cut it in that line of work. Or Joanne. Or Brenda."

"So, her name used to be Joan, Joanne or Brenda, and she changed it to Lavender?"

"No," said Puffs, rolling his eyes. "Those were examples. We're just saying that the person writing you these notes must be old enough to change her name. She must be over eighteen."

"And she's not a doctor," said Rooster. "Or a lawyer."

"Or a dentist," said Puffs.

"Or a real estate agent," said Rooster.

Puffs hesitated after that one. "She could be a real estate agent."

"You think so?"

"Uh-huh. That could be a name you see on a sign selling real estate. Lavender. Lavender McLeod, something like that. 'For a great deal, call me, Lavender McLeod. I'll put you where you want to be.'"

"I'll bet she would," said Rooster, as an aside.

"I think that's believable," said Puffs.

"All right then." Rooster looked back at Puffs. "There you go. She's either a table dancer, a stripper or a real estate agent. Take your pick."

Jayson had been overwhelmed by the idea of having a secret admirer, especially such a flamboyant one. Rooster and Puffs eventually told him it was a gag. He'd been vowing revenge ever since.

"Jayson will make you guys pay for that. He will make you pay big-time."

"Take a joke already," said Rooster, tired of the threats.

"The Jay-man is on alert. He will conquer."

Rooster met Jolene in grade nine. She had just moved to Winston from Ottawa with her mom and dad and her little sister, Raquel. She arrived at the high school in November. She was small, thin and had big lively eyes and soft pale skin. She kept to herself and had made only a few friends by the time Rooster's eyes found her shortly before Christmas.

"Who's that?" he said to Jayson one day in the cafeteria.

"Who's what?" said Jayson, devouring his lunch.

"That girl over there. With the brown hair."

Jayson turned and looked over his shoulder. "That's Tammy Kyle."

"Not her. The other one. The little one in the blue sweater over there."

"Oh. That's Lindy Raymond. I play volleyball with her brother."

"Are you an idiot? I know who Tammy Kyle and Lindy Raymond are. I'm looking at that little blue girl over there with the empty tray in her hand. She just got butted out of line."

"Where?"

"I just told you where."

"Jayson doesn't see a little blue girl anywhere. Oh, now he does. Jayson knows her. She's in his math class."

"What's her name?"

"Jayson doesn't know."

"She's cute."

Jayson shrugged his shoulders. "Jayson's pretty big on Belinda MacPherson at the moment. He's gonna ask her to go to the dance with him this Friday."

Rooster took his eyes off Jolene and frowned at Jayson. "Belinda MacPherson?"

"Uh-huh."

"She eats her lunch with her mouth open, you know that? Puffs told me about it the other day and we watched her."

"Jayson likes her. He couldn't care less how she eats her lunch."

"The way you eat, that's probably true. I like that chick over there. What's her name again?"

"Jayson doesn't know. Jolene, maybe."

"Jolene?"

Jayson nodded and chewed another bite of his sandwich. "Something weird like that."

In spite of his cocksure ways, Rooster was not a natural when it came to girls. He had never had a steady girlfriend. He'd made out with Casey Tatum in grade eight, at a party, and he had almost undone Tanya Smyl's bra one hot afternoon in the summer between grades eight and nine. When her mother came home unexpectedly, Rooster had been forced to hide under Tanya's bed until her mom went back to work, at which point Tanya broke up with him, saying he was bad luck and too clumsy.

"What's so clumsy about me?" he had said on his way out the door.

"What's so clumsy? My God. I can undo my bra in my sleep. It felt like you had boxing gloves on, the way you were doing it."

His only other fling with romance occurred at Christmas break when he was fourteen. He met Jayson's cousin, Louisa, at a tobogganing party. She was visiting with her parents from Saskatoon. She had flaming red hair and freckles all over her hands and face.

"You should see me in the summer," she said after everyone had returned to Jayson's house for pizza. "I have them all over my arms, my legs, my back."

"I'd love to see that," said Rooster, whose bravery was enhanced by the flask of whiskey and Coke that Jayson's older brother, Russell, had smuggled to the tobogganing hill. "Let's set it up."

"You're drunk," said Louisa, shoving him away.

"You are not," said Rooster. "I mean, I am not."

On her final day in Winston, Louisa confessed to Rooster, stone sober with a headache, that she did in fact have a crush on him, but she also had a boyfriend back home.

"Marvin wants to be a boxer," she said. "He works out every day in the gym. You should see him hit the speed bag."

"She liked me, though," Rooster said to his friends after she'd left. "You could see it in her eyes."

"She had a cold," said Jayson. "Her eyes were running all week. She couldn't stop blowing her nose."

"She told me she had a crush on me."

"She was being nice," said Puffs. "She felt sorry for you."

Rooster asked Jolene out after school the next day. It was an awkward moment for him, especially with Puffs and Jayson lurking around the corner. Jolene told him she would think about it and get back to him before the dance on Friday.

"You sure knocked her out," said Puffs.

The next afternoon, she stopped him in the hallway and said yes, she would like to go out with him, providing he met her parents first. "And they're super strict," she said, "so be ready."

Mrs. Delaney answered the door when Rooster rang the bell early Friday evening. She was a short stout woman, with glasses attached to a gold chain around her neck and a thick novel in her hand. Her face fell into a frown as soon as she saw him.

"You are...?" she said after giving him the once-over.

"Rooster Cobb. I'm here to take Jolene to the dance tonight." He had done his best to pull himself together. His hair, usually spiked high with gel, was slicked neatly to the side. He wore a white shirt buttoned to the collar. His blue jeans were clean, and he had taken a Kleenex to the toes of his black boots before leaving the house.

Mrs. Delaney invited him inside. "That's a very interesting name you have, Rooster. Why don't you tell me about it?"

Rooster smiled to himself. The story was one of his favorites. "When I was a kid, like, really little, I used to go and stand on the end of my parents' bed and make noises until they woke up. One day, my dad told me I reminded him of a goddamn rooster."

Mrs. Delaney continued to frown. "He didn't have a problem using that kind of language in front of his children?"

"I'm an only child, so I guess it didn't matter."

Mr. Delaney joined them a short time later. He was a tall, regal-looking man with a neatly trimmed beard and mustache. He wore a dark brown cardigan and corduroy pants. He, too, was holding a book. Behind them, in the background, Rooster could hear classical music coming from the stereo.

"Conroy Delaney, son." Mr. Delaney extended his hand and nearly crushed Rooster's fingers. "A man is only as good as his word and his handshake. That's what my father used to say." His voice was strong and clear and used to being listened to.

"You should hear the language this boy's father uses around him," said Mrs. Delaney.

"Fill their ears with goodness and they will grow up to be good," said Mr. Delaney before Rooster could explain that his father was no longer living.

"Tell him where your name comes from. No, on second thought, don't bother. He'll only get upset."

"You can tell me what you plan on doing with my daughter tonight. I hope that doesn't make me upset."

Rooster said something about just going to the dance and maybe taking a little walk after.

"After what, son?"

"The dance?"

"And what time will that be?"

Rooster shrugged his shoulders. "I'm not sure. Ten? Eleven?"

"No, it won't be that time." Mr. Delaney shook his head, in unison with Mrs. Delaney.

"It won't?"

"It won't be ten and it won't be eleven. It will be nine thirty, and you'll be right back where you are right now or you won't be seeing our daughter again."

"Oh. Okay."

"Is that understood?"

"Yup."

"I beg your pardon?"

"I said yup, I get it. Nine thirty, right back here."

They hit it off at the dance, and for the next two years Rooster saw Jolene at school every day and occasionally on weekends. The reason they did not spend more time together was that Mr. and Mrs. Delaney did not share her sentiments for him.

"My mommy and daddy don't like you, you know," said Jolene's sister, Raquel, one day. She was seven years younger than Jolene.

"They don't like you, either," said Rooster. The two of them were alone in the kitchen while Jolene finished getting ready upstairs. The babysitter had not yet arrived for Raquel. Mr. and Mrs. Delaney had gone out for the night.

"Yes, they do."

"That's not what I heard."

"They do so!"

"Not as much as they like me."

"They don't like you at all."

"They don't like you at *all*, at all."

"I'm telling on you."

"I'm telling on *you*."

Jolene was clearly different from most of the other girls he knew. She did not smoke and she rarely swore. At parties, whenever she was allowed to go to one, she drank Coke or water with a twist of lemon. She read novels like *Jane Eyre*, by Charlotte Bronte, and *Pride and Prejudice*, by Jane Austen. She encouraged Rooster to write more and even suggested one day when they were home alone in her living room that he join the staff of the student newspaper and become a reporter.

"Deadlines make me crazy," he had replied. "I could never do that."

"You're just chicken, that's what it is," she said back.

"No, I'm not. I don't even like writing. Why would I do that?"

"Because you're good at it, that's why. And you do so like it. You just don't want to admit it. It's not cool enough for you."

"Well, okay. So I don't want to admit it. What's the big deal?"

"If you're good at something, you should at least give it a try."

"Maybe someday I will." He put his arm around her shoulder. "But anyway, shouldn't we be making out or something? Can't we save this conversation for when your parents get home, or that irritating little sister of yours, at least?"

From the beginning of their time together, Rooster was never exactly sure what it was that he liked most about her. She could be feisty, funny, cranky and smart. She liked to kiss and touch, but she made it clear from the beginning that she would not be going all the way until she was much older.

"Do you know what my dad would do if he caught us in bed together?" she said one night.

"Do you know what *my* dad would do if your dad caught us in bed together?" said Rooster.

"Your dad's dead."

"Exactly. He'd say, 'Welcome to heaven, Rooster. What did you go and do a dumb thing like that for?'"

Near the end of grade eleven, the Delaneys realized that their daughter had not gotten into any real trouble during her time with Rooster. Her marks had not suffered (which had been one of the conditions for her seeing him at all), and really, around them at least, he was not a bad kid. That is, he was very well-mannered whenever they had him over for supper, and he was always cordial at the door and polite on the phone.

"We just wish he had a little more *ambition*," said Mrs. Delaney one night at the dinner table.

"A young man must have drive before he can steer his way to the future," said Mr. Delaney. "A man who knows, goes. We never hear him talk about what he wants to be when he grows up. Where he wants to go to school."

"You never talk to him about anything," said Jolene in Rooster's defense. "You have him over here, but you never say anything to him."

"What we're saying, honey, is that we never hear you talk about him that way." Mrs. Delaney smiled patiently. "We don't want to see you held *down* by anyone, especially now. My goodness. Grade twelve awaits you, and then it's on to the world!" She beamed at her daughter. "It's an exciting time for you and for Rooster too, we hope."

"He should really think about changing his name," said Mr. Delaney, as a final thought on the subject before dessert. "I don't see myself hiring a young man named Rooster to work in my department, and I don't think I'm alone in that."

Jolene shook her head. "I don't think Rooster will ever change his name. He got it from his father."

Rooster walked for about an hour along the path in the ravine. Out of boredom, he smoked one cigarette after another. The dominant thought on his mind was that Jolene would be mad at him for skipping again. She'd been on him a lot for that lately, to the point where it was starting to bother him.

"You're starting to sound like your mother, you know," he'd said to her recently. "Pretty soon you'll start sounding like your dad. 'Son, a young man who walks away from learning ends up with sore feet and an empty head. You can't go if you don't know.'"

"I don't care. It's time to stop skipping so much."

"Says who?"

"Says anyone with a brain big enough to figure out that skipping school so close to graduation is not a good idea."

"Well, I think it's time to skip *more*. This time next year I won't be in school. I won't be able to skip at all."

Jolene shook her head. "That's a really good theory, Rooster." There were times when she thought a lot like her mother too.

"I think it makes sense."

"Well, it won't make much sense if you're back in school again next year, now will it?"

She had a point there, and he knew it. He also knew that with Puffs doing so well with his computer business, and Jayson on the verge of becoming an even bigger star athlete or making tons of money on his father's construction crew, and with Jolene focusing so hard on getting into university, he was the one most likely to be left behind.

That was the thought that scared him most when he thought of his days ahead: being left behind while his friends went on to make something of themselves. It was also the one he tried hardest not to think about.

He knew it was a problem that he would have to deal with someday, though.

He also knew that his meeting with Mrs. Nixon the next morning, whatever it was about, would not solve anything. He did not see himself walking out of her office with a sudden love for learning, or a burning desire to do as well as he possibly could in his remaining classes.

He had seen her too many times already to believe anything like that was about to happen.

3

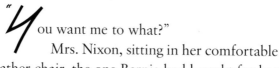

"*Y*ou want me to what?"

Mrs. Nixon, sitting in her comfortable black leather chair, the one Bernie had bought for her two years ago, covered her mouth and pretended to cough. Really, she was smiling and did not want Rooster to see. The two of them were sitting in her office. It was shortly after nine o'clock, and she had just told him about the plan involving himself, the Strikers and the bowling alley. She was quietly delighted with his reaction.

"Mrs. Helmsley and I agree that it's a good idea. We think it will give you a chance to ... "

"Say it again. You want me to what?" Rooster leaned forward in his chair so he could hear her better. Her office was small, tidy and full of books on counseling, addiction and coping with troubled teens. Adorning the walls were pictures of her and Bernie skiing on a gloriously snowy mountain in Whistler, B.C., sharing a laugh and a kiss at a beach resort in Maui, and posing with their golden retriever, Nana, named after the lovable dog in *Peter Pan*.

Mrs. Nixon cleared her throat and told him again what they wanted him to do.

"Are you serious?"

She nodded. "Absolutely."

"And you think I'm actually going to do this?"

"We think you actually want to graduate, and we know your mother wants you to do this because we know she wants you to graduate."

"You talked to my mother?"

"I did. About fifteen minutes ago."

"What did you tell her?"

"I told her everything. The whole story."

"Which is what?"

"Which is that you had better get your act together in a hurry or else you'll be back in here again next year or out on your own without a grade twelve diploma. That's the truth, Rooster. That's the way it is for you right now."

Rooster shook his head. "And this is your version of helping me out? Supervising a bunch of clowns at a bowling alley?"

"No one said they were clowns."

"Whatever. This is your bright idea?"

"As a matter of fact, it is, yes. This is my bright idea. Mrs. Helmsley had input. She chose you for it, actually. I was thinking of someone else entirely."

"Who?"

"Well, I had thought that someone like Ainsley Miller would have been good for it, or Mackenzie Ashcroff."

"Ainsley Miller or Mackenzie Ashcroff?"

"Uh-huh."

"They're, like, the smartest kids in the whole school."

"That's right."

"How did you ever go from them to me?"

"I didn't. Mrs. Helmsley thought of it. She turned my idea from being a learning opportunity for our finest students to a final opportunity for you. After thinking about it, I see her point. This is your last chance, Rooster. We're doing you a favor."

Rooster stared at her for a moment. In spite of all their quarrels in the past, he had never actually disliked Mrs. Nixon. But at this moment, he disliked her very very much.

"Well, I'm not doing it." He sat back in his chair and crossed his arms. "I'm not going to take a bunch of people I don't even know down to the bowling alley and sit there and watch them bowl. I don't even like bowling. It's a stupid sport and I'm lousy at it. So forget it. I'm not gonna do it, and there's nothing in the world that's gonna make me change my mind."

Mrs. Nixon held her ground. "Yes, you are doing it, Rooster."

"No way."

"You're going to meet them today after school."

"Uh-uh."

"You have only yourself to blame for being in this situation. Defiance is not going to help you here."

"Oh no?"

"No, it's not."

"What is then?"

"I beg your pardon?"

"What is going to help me?"

"Well..." Mrs. Nixon had to think for a moment. The reason she had added counseling to her portfolio as a teacher was so she could get to know her students better and do more for them. The courses she had taken gave her fresh insights into a young person's world and new perspectives on communication and relationships. True, it was more work being a counselor and a teacher, but she loved it. She absolutely loved her job, in spite of her occasional objections to Mrs. Helmsley's ways, and she loved working at Winston High. Right at this second, however, she was in a helluva jam. What skills and abilities did Rooster Cobb have that would help him serve as a team leader to a group of mentally handicapped adults who wished to go bowling once a week? She smiled and cleared her throat. Compounding the problem was the simple fact that for every tick on the clock that she had to think about it, the credibility of what she came up with was reduced.

"Well, Rooster." She shifted her position in her chair. "When you put your mind to it…"

Someone knocked on her door. Before she could say anything, Mrs. Helmsley walked in. "How's it going?" Her presence filled the room immediately, like an airplane wedging itself into a two-car garage. "He's all for it, I'm sure? Ready to go?"

"Not quite," said Mrs. Nixon. "At the moment, as a matter of fact, he's wondering what skills he has that we think make him suitable for the job."

Mrs. Helmsley turned the full force of her attention to Rooster, who remained slouched in his chair, but slightly less slouched than he had been when he was alone with Mrs. Nixon.

"Skills?" said Mrs. Helmsley. "This isn't about matching you with something we know you can do, young man. This is a challenge. This is about seeing whether or not you have the courage to stand up to something new, take it on and excel at it. It's for *you* to show *us* what skills you have, not the other way around."

Rooster looked briefly at Mrs. Nixon, then back into the blinding glare of Mrs. Helmsley. "Well, forget it then," he said. "I told her I wasn't going to do it, and I'll say the same thing to you. Find someone else."

Mrs. Helmsley stared at Rooster for another moment, then she looked at Mrs. Nixon, then back at Rooster. "All right," she said finally. "Get out."

Rooster began to lift himself off the chair. "Finally someone who actually listens to me around here."

"But if you go now, you leave this office, you leave this school and you never come back. Not this year, not next year, not the year after that. You're through." She spoke with the power and clarity of a judge sentencing a criminal. "We've broken our backs for you in here. We've put up with your bad behavior, your poor performance, your disrespect. Not anymore. If you get off that chair and leave this office, you're done. That's it."

Rooster froze in mid-motion. The game had changed to hardball, as his stepdad, Irving, would say, and he was woefully unprepared for it.

Mrs. Helmsley continued. "It's not my wish to fill my hometown with high-school dropouts. But I am not going to stand here and watch you walk away from an opportunity to get it right, for the first time in your life, and say nothing. That's not my style. So go now and be done for good, or stick around and try to make something of yourself. Take your pick."

Rooster hesitated. He wanted to leave. He wanted to walk away from Helmsley and her stupid power trips, but he knew there would be severe consequences. His mother would have a fit; Jolene might never speak to him again. Even the guys might think he had made a dumb decision, although he wasn't sure about that one yet. Still, he knew he would regret it.

Slowly, painfully, he lowered himself back into his chair.

"That's a very good idea." Mrs. Helmsley watched him sit down. "That shows what we've suspected all along. You have a brain; you just don't like to use it."

He remained silent.

"Mrs. Nixon will fill you in on the details. But let me add this." She pointed a rigid finger at Rooster's head. "No funny stuff. I want to see effort, commitment and respect from you, and when this is over, I want to hear from the staff at Common House that the people you were working with are better off because of you and what you've added to their lives. Do you understand that?"

Rooster barely nodded his head once.

"Good." Mrs. Helmsley left the office. A moment of silence followed.

Then, "We're to meet them at four fifteen down there," said Mrs. Nixon. "The four people you'll be most involved with have prepared an interview for you."

Rooster shifted his gaze from a small spot on Mrs. Nixon's desk, which he had been staring at absently, to her face. "An interview?"

"That's right."

"What for?"

"I'm not sure. I think it's to determine whether or not they want to work with you."

"Whether or not *they* want to work with *me*?"

"That's right."

A small amount of life returned to his features. "You mean they have a choice?"

"Apparently, yes, they do."

He straightened himself in his chair. The deep crease in his forehead from frowning began to disappear. "So, if they don't take me, I'm out of this?"

Mrs. Nixon shook her head. "It's not that easy, Rooster."

"You can't force them to take me."

"No."

"And if the majority votes against me....We live in a democratic society, Mrs. Nixon. You can't go against the majority."

Mrs. Nixon sat back in her chair and crossed her arms. "So you actually did learn something in social studies."

"Of course."

"I wonder if your teacher, Mr. Standford, knows that."

"He never asks the right questions on the exams."

"Uh-huh."

"But it's true though, right? If three of the four say *forget it*, there's nothing you or Mrs. Helmsley or anyone else can do about it."

"I would not go there today with the intent of blowing off the interview, Rooster."

"It's a personality thing. Sometimes you click, sometimes you don't. Look at you and Bernie."

"Leave it alone, Rooster."

"I know you guys clicked, but I'm sure there were lots of other girls looking his way. Maybe he liked a few of them too, but obviously not as much as you. Unless…"

"You've gone far enough," said Mrs. Nixon.

"Hey, I didn't mean to bring up something you don't want to talk about."

"Drop it, now."

"You always seem happy talking about him. I guess I thought that was really how you felt."

"I will see you at four o'clock at the front doors of Common House. Be there on time. Look presentable. Be prepared to show them the best possible version of you."

Rooster stood up. He could barely restrain his glee. "It may not be enough. That's all I'm saying."

"Goodbye, Rooster." Mrs. Nixon remained seated in her chair.

"I'm sorry if I upset you. I had no idea there were problems in your relationship with Bernie."

"There are no problems in my relationship with my husband."

"All right. If you say so."

"I say so."

"Well, that's good then. That's the way it should be."

"Goodbye, Rooster," she said again.

"My point is, if there was a panel of four people voting on whether you should marry Bernie, and three of the four said no, then you'd be sitting here with pictures of you and someone else having all this fun.

Right?" He motioned toward the photographs on her walls and desk.

Mrs. Nixon held his stare evenly. She did not move her head side to side or up and down. She waited until Rooster finally left, then she relaxed. How would she have fared had Bernie's mother and father and his younger sister been given a chance to vote on their decision to marry? She contemplated that question for a moment. Then, when the answer became clear, she dropped it and prepared to go teach her ten o'clock class.

4

*R*ooster's mother, Eunice, was an excitable type. She drank copious amounts of coffee, or Coke if she wanted a change. "Omigod!" was how she frequently started a conversation or, depending on the situation, added to an existing one. She knew something about everyone in their neighborhood.

Her favorite spot in their small cluttered house was next to the large window by the kitchen table, where she would sit for long stretches at a time, especially on the weekends, and either watch the world go by or think. Her forehead was creased down the middle from constant worry.

During the week, she was a receptionist at a small, locally owned insurance company—Smith Insurance. She worked from eight thirty to four thirty, five days a week, with an hour off for lunch, during which she and a colleague would put on their running shoes, when the weather was nice, and go for a lengthy talk-filled walk.

Eunice had long dark hair that fell straight to her shoulders. She was medium height and thin. Like her son, she was a smoker, and in spite of her best efforts, she always found that quitting was much harder than it looked.

Across from her at the table, on a typical weekend morning, reading the sports pages while he ate, or looking out the window with her when he was done reading, was Irving, her second husband. Irving was a big man, with forearms the diameter of small trees, and shoulders that were powerfully round and thick. He stood six feet five inches tall and tipped the scales at 260. In his day, his playing weight had been around 215 or 225 at the start of spring training.

Irving had been a pitcher. He'd had a so-so fastball, a decent curveball and a slider that never quite fulfilled itself the way he had hoped. "I was one more decent pitch away from making my mark in the bigs," he would say to Rooster and his friends whenever he had the chance. "You need three pitches to survive up there, or one terrific one, like a Roger Clemens fastball, or a Niekro knuckleball, but them knuckleballers are a breed apart anyway, so they don't count. But even the Rocket had other stuff he could throw if his fastball wasn't working. You need a setup pitch, y'know. You gotta get that guy standing up there with a stick in his hands to think, 'Now what's he gonna throw at me this time?' If he's not thinkin' that, if he's up there sittin' on the only pitch you got, unless it's one helluva pitch, you're not gonna be up there very long."

"Is that why you weren't up there very long?" said Rooster one day.

"That is precisely the reason," said Irving, who spoke honestly about himself and others. "I had a good fastball, a decent curveball, but my slider didn't slide for me the way I wanted her to." He also repeated himself a lot. "And unless you've got three special pitches, or one terrific one, forget it. You'll be there long enough to have a cuppa coffee, and then it's goodbye."

Irving's career ran from 1971, when he was twenty years old, until 1984, when he finally hung up his glove for good. He was, in baseball parlance, a career minor leaguer, with one brief, unforgettable exception, in 1979, when he was called up by the then woeful Minnesota Twins to bolster their injury-depleted and inept pitching staff.

His record was one win and three losses, with a total of nine appearances in thirty-one games.

He met Eunice in the fall of 2000, three years after the death of her first husband, Rooster's father, Michael Cobb. They met through a mutual friend. Eunice knew nothing about baseball. She had played softball at school because she had to, and by the time

she met Irving, she had not held a bat in her hands,
or watched even an inning of a game, in well over a
decade.

By that time, however, Irving was well into the
post-baseball phase of his life, which, like his pitching
career, had not gone quite the way he had planned it.
He'd been married and divorced. He'd tried his hand
at coaching, but the relentless travel and poor pay
wore him down. He'd gone back to school to complete
the college degree that he had set aside to pursue his
baseball career, but left again when he discovered the
level of commitment and work that was required. He'd
started a small business with a friend from high school
and then went bankrupt. He'd worked construction
but hurt his back when he lost his balance one day and
fell off a roof he was framing.

Irving was not one to mope when such endeavors
failed to go his way, though, or to shake his fist at the
world for treating him unfairly. For Eunice, that was
all she needed to see to fall for him.

"He's what I need," she told a friend during the relatively peaceful days of courtship. "He's a good, honest
man. He has a sense of humor."

Her friend, Dolores, from the office, did not agree.
"He's bringing nothing to the relationship, Eunice.
He has no job. No money. Does he even have a fixed
address?"

"He loves to read and go for walks."

"That's because he doesn't work. He has nothing

else to do. And the sports pages do not count as reading. I'm sorry."

"He's been through a lot, and he doesn't talk about it the way other people would. He's not bitter or disappointed. He sees there's more to life than just making money."

"He's a loser, Eunice. I hate to say it, but don't you dare marry that man."

"I don't think Rooster likes him very much, though. They haven't bonded the way I'd hoped."

"I won't even comment on that."

Eunice was twelve years younger than Irving. On their wedding day, he was fifty and she was thirty-eight. Puffs, Jayson and Rooster had all been in the wedding party, along with a couple of the boys from Irving's playing days.

After the short, informal ceremony, they had gone to the local baseball diamond for pictures. Eunice put on a baseball cap (the Chicago Cubs, Irving's favorite team) for the first time in her life, and Irving scooped her up in his arms and carried her around the bases.

Jayson thought it was the coolest wedding he'd ever been to, but Rooster expressed a different opinion. "I have to call this clown my dad now?"

"Call him Irving," said Puffs. "He's not your dad."

Rooster nodded in agreement. "You got that right."

Unexpectedly, Rooster's mom was standing in the kitchen when he arrived home after school. Usually she was still at work.

Sensing trouble, Rooster went immediately on the offensive. "Well, thanks a lot for getting me into this mess," he said, kicking his shoes off. "Instead of studying tonight, I get to go bowling. No, first I get to meet my new friends. Then I get to go bowling."

"I got you into this mess?" said his mom, her arms crossed firmly in front of her chest.

"You agreed to it. That's what Mrs. Nixon said."

"Listen, bub. No one got you into anything but yourself. You've been dogging it all year."

"That's not true."

"It is true."

"No it's not."

"I got off the phone with your teacher and I looked over at Dolores and said, 'Omigod. Rooster's failing every class he's in. He's not going to graduate this year.'"

"Let me guess. She said, 'Go easy on the poor kid, Eunice. He's a sweetheart. Don't worry about him so much.'"

"Dolores said what she always says whenever your name comes up. 'Get rid of him. You don't need that worry in your life. Let him see what it's really like out there.'"

Rooster moved toward the refrigerator. "Dolores is a hag, Mom. You should really stop talking to her. And I'm not failing every course. I'm passing English."

"She's not a hag. She's my friend and she's right."

"She's a hag." He opened the fridge door. "Where's that leftover pizza from last night?"

Rooster

From his post by the window, with the most recent edition of *Baseball Today* spread out before him, Irving cleared his throat and patted his thick stomach. "It's right down here, young fella. I had it for lunch about two, three hours ago."

Rooster's shoulders sagged. "All of it?"

"Every bit. Those boys down there at Little Tony's know how to put one together. Make yourself a sandwich if you want. There's cold cuts there in the meat drawer. Bread's right behind you on the counter."

"I don't want a sandwich," said Rooster, still staring into the fridge. "I wanted pizza."

"Well, there's cheese in there. Put a little of that on a piece of bread. Put it in the microwave for a minute. There you go. Poor man's pizza. Good as gold. You can slice some onion on it too, if you want. Put a little ham on the top."

"Why didn't you have the poor man's pizza and leave the real pizza for me?"

"It's not that good," said Irving, turning the page of his paper. "It's good in a pinch, but it's not as good as the real thing."

Rooster shook his head. It was not the first time that all the good leftovers had disappeared before he returned home from school. "How come I'm always the guy in a pinch? I worked hard at school all day. I should be coming home to a real pizza."

"Excuse me?" said his mom, getting back into the action.

"What?"

"Did you say you worked hard at school all day?"

"Yes."

"Are you kidding me?"

"Hey, I work hard." He closed the fridge door.

"Not according to your teacher you don't. She said you haven't done much at all lately."

"First of all, she's not my teacher, all right. She's that young counselor you don't like, Mrs. Nixon. Second, I'm in her office today and I have to start explaining what a democracy is to her because she doesn't know."

"What counselor that I don't like?"

"The young one. She wears all those fancy clothes all the time? You were in to see her last semester about that book report I did, and you walked out saying she was too young to be a counselor. You didn't think she was old enough to know anything. You said that to her face, as a matter of fact."

"It was her I was talking to today?"

"Uh-huh."

"I didn't know it was her I was talking to."

"See? She always makes everything sound ten times worse than it really is, remember? You said that yourself last year."

"And she's got you involved with this bowling team?"

"That's her big idea. She thinks I have to prove myself. That I have to show I'm worth graduating."

"Are there other kids involved in this?"

"No. I'm the only kid in the whole school who has to do it. But get this—the other two kids she was thinking of asking were Ainsley Miller and Mackenzie Ashcroff."

"Who are they?"

"The two smartest kids in the school, by far. So does that not mean that she thinks I can do what they can do? She has me up there with, like, Einstein and whoever, but she tells you I'm flunking out. Why? Because she wanted you to say yes to making me do it."

Eunice had to think for a moment. "Why is she so anxious to make you do this?"

Rooster gave an exaggerated shrug. "Ask her. I don't know. She doesn't like me, I know that for sure. Maybe she just wants to make things difficult. I mean, would it not be smarter to say, 'Rooster, clear off everything from your schedule. You have to study hard every night from now until finals'? Does she do that? No. She gives me a new project to work on."

"I remember her now," said his mom, nodding.

"You know she doesn't like me. I'm not feeding you a line here. You know she doesn't like me."

She continued to nod and to think.

"But don't worry about this bowling thing," continued Rooster. "I'll take care of that. I'll be out of that in half an hour."

"How?"

"They want me to go there today at four fifteen to interview for a job I don't want. So I'm just going to go there and say, 'Hey listen. I don't have time for this, all right? I would like my marks to be better. Final exams are next month. Would it be a great idea for me to take this on right now? No. I'm sorry.'"

"You think that'll be enough?"

"I don't think I should have to do a job if I don't want to do it."

"And are you actually going to study now that final exams are only a few weeks away?"

"Mom, this happens every year. Every year you have a panic attack about my grades, and every year I ace the finals and move on. Every year."

"I wouldn't say you ace them."

"I do well enough to pass. How's that?"

Eunice hesitated for a moment. She still had some thoughts to sort out. But for now she was satisfied and not nearly as anxious or upset as she had been after Mrs. Nixon's phone call. "Okay," she said. "Come straight home afterward. You can start your studying tonight." She looked at Irving. "I'll be back in a minute. I'm going to change out of my work clothes." She left the kitchen.

Rooster said goodbye and opened the fridge again. He was in a hurry now, but he was also still hungry.

"So that's your plan, is it?" said Irving, still sitting by the window. "Get out of the bowling and hope like hell you can pass the finals?"

Rooster pulled the peanut butter and the jam from the fridge and shut the door with his foot. "Yeah, that's my plan," he said, moving quickly.

Irving flipped another page. "Well, for your sake, I hope it works."

"It has every year. There's no reason it should fail me now." He smeared a thick layer of peanut butter on one piece of bread and a large plop of strawberry jam on the other.

"You know what your mother's big concern is, don't you?" Irving was looking at Rooster now instead of his paper.

"Uh, that I graduate from high school?" Rooster returned the jars to the fridge and scooped up his sandwich from the counter.

"No, it's not that."

Rooster dug his feet into his shoes and prepared to leave. "What is it then?"

"It's that you don't end up like me."

Rooster stopped at the back door. "What?" he said.

"She doesn't say it quite like that, but that's what she's thinking. That you'll end up just like me if you don't get your act together. The thing is, you won't be just like me, 'cause at least I had a talent in something. I could pitch. I could throw a baseball, at least."

"Not very well."

"Twenty years as a professional baseball player? I'd say that's pretty well. Not well enough for the majors, unfortunately for me, but I'll take what I had. I did okay."

Rooster turned toward the door. "If you say so."

"You bet your life I say so. There's ten million people out there who'd drop everything in a second to experience for one month what I had for nearly two decades. You—you won't have that. You keep jacking around now, settling for doing 'well enough to pass,' you'll be sitting here looking out the window just like I am, but you won't have twenty years' worth of memories to carry you through. You won't have anything."

Rooster hesitated before leaving.

"You think about that as you carry out this plan of yours. Maybe that woman from your school is onto something with this group of people who want to go bowling. I don't know what it is, but maybe she knows something."

"I doubt that very much."

Irving shrugged and returned to his paper. "It's something to think about," he said. "Just know that if your plan doesn't work, you won't be the only person in this kitchen right now to fail."

Rooster did not respond. He let the screen door slam on his way out.

5

C ommon House was a good twenty-minute walk, most of it uphill, from Rooster's home. He was tired and out of breath by the time he arrived. Mrs. Nixon was waiting for him.

"You're late," she said, holding the door open. "You look pale," she added as he stepped inside.

"I am pale. All the blood ran to my feet walking up that stupid hill."

She immediately led him into an office where five people were seated around a circular table. One of them, a tall, middle-aged woman with dark, neatly combed hair and a pleasant smile, rose to meet him. "Rooster, I'm Mrs. Yuler. Pleased to meet you. These are the Strikers." She waved her hand toward the others at the table. "Have a seat, please. We can get started."

Rooster remained standing. "Actually, I was kinda hoping I could go for a quick smoke before meeting with everyone. I'm pretty nervous. I've never been in an interview like this before. I've never had a job, so ... this is all pretty new to me. I wouldn't mind a minute to settle down."

Mrs. Yuler looked at him in surprise. Behind him, sitting in a chair in the corner of the office so she was not a part of the interview but was still close enough to observe it, Mrs. Nixon shook her head.

"Well," said Mrs. Yuler, looking at her watch, "we did say four fifteen, and it's actually four thirty already. Four thirty-three to be exact."

"I know," said Rooster, with a shrug but no apology. "I got hung up at home. The old man ate all my supper, so I had to scramble for something to eat. Drank all my beer too."

"Didn't the walk here give you time to calm down and ... have a smoke?"

He shook his head. "Way too strenuous. That goddamn hill out there almost killed me. I don't know how these guys get up and down that stupid thing all the time." He motioned toward the Strikers. "I'm glad I'm not fat, that's all I can say."

"We live here," said one of the members of the team, a woman with a pile of brown hair and very thick glasses. "We don't have to go up and down it unless we're in the van."

"The goddamn hill," said the woman next to her.

She was short and squat with greasy black hair. She also wore glasses, but they were so filthy that Rooster could barely see her eyes through them. "That's a good one. Heh, heh. I'm gonna remember that one. Heh, heh. Goddamn hill."

"Roseann," said Mrs. Yuler sternly.

"Sorry," said the woman with the greasy hair. She immediately sank down in her chair and began licking her fingers. "I'm sorry. I won't do it again."

"Just watch your language."

"I'm sorry. He started it. He said goddamn hill before I did."

"I know. I'll have to talk with him about that after."

"He started it." She continued to lick her fingers. Her voice was deep and hard, like a man's voice.

"I know who started it, Roseann."

"It wasn't me."

"You be the one to end it."

"It wasn't me who started it. He said goddamn hill before I did. I'm sorry. I won't do it again."

"That's good. I believe you."

Rooster stared at Roseann in shock.

"You got her into trouble," said the woman who had spoken first.

"It was an accident," said Mrs. Yuler. "I'm sure that was a sign of the nervousness that Rooster spoke about. I doubt he talks like that all the time."

"No, he doesn't," said Mrs. Nixon, from the corner. "And if he knows what's good for him, he won't talk like that again. Now sit down, Rooster. The interview has started."

Rooster reluctantly sat down. He had not meant to get anyone in trouble, but he was more determined than ever to stick with his plan.

"Okay then," said Mrs. Yuler. "Let's start with introductions, shall we? Everyone, you already know this is Rooster. Rooster, this is Roseann, who you just met. Beside her is Dorothy-Jane-Anne. Next to her is Tim. Next to Tim is Percival. They are the Strikers." She smiled. Rooster offered a small tight smile back. "They have questions for you, I know. Now who would like to go first? Tim? Maybe you'd like to begin?"

Tim was extremely thin and sat hunched in his chair like an old man in a wheelchair. When she mentioned his name, he quickly sat up straight. His big wide eyes sprang to life. His voice burst with energy and excitement. "Okay, okay. All right. I'll ask the first question. I'll get things started." He rubbed his hands together and began to rock back and forth in his chair. "All right then. Rooster, I'm ready to fire away! Oh boy. I've been waiting a long time for this. I've been waiting for this for a long long time."

"Tim," said Mrs. Yuler patiently. "Just ask the question."

"Okay, okay. All right then. Here we go, boy. Here we go. Rock 'n' roll. That's what I like to say. Okay. I would like to know, I would like to know if you like pizza."

Rooster, anticipating something more challenging, hesitated before answering. How can I screw this up enough to get out of here? he thought to himself.

"Any kind," said Tim, still rocking in his chair. "Pepperoni. Ham and pineapple. Super deluxe. Black olives. Tomatoes. Green peppers. You name it. Any kind. Any kind at all."

"Cheese," said Roseann, cutting in. "That's the best kind."

"No it's not," said Dorothy-Jane-Anne, staring at Rooster.

"Yes," said Roseann.

"No."

"It is so."

"No it's not."

"Ladies," said Mrs. Yuler, "stay out of it. Let Rooster answer the question. You will all get a chance to talk."

Rooster cleared his throat. "Uhm." He still wasn't sure what to say. "What was the question again?"

"I would like to know if…do you like pizza?" said Tim. "Any kind. Any kind at all. Any kind they can make."

In truth, pizza was Rooster's favorite food on earth, which is why he was so frustrated every time Irving ate all the leftovers. "I like leftover pizza," he said suddenly. "I like cold pizza. I hate it when it's hot. It burns my mouth all the time."

Tim frowned and stopped rocking in his chair. Roseann pulled her right index finger out of her mouth. Dorothy-Jane-Anne continued to stare at him.

"You don't like hot pizza?" said Tim.

"Hate it."

"It burns your mouth?" said Dorothy-Jane-Anne.

"The pizza sauce. It's so hot sometimes. I don't know. It's messy too. When it's cold, the toppings don't slide around so much. They just sit there on top of the crust. It's way easier to eat it when it's cold. I don't know why people eat it hot all the time. That makes no sense to me. It's not half as good as when it's cold." Happy with his answer and the looks he was getting because of it, Rooster relaxed in his chair and crossed his arms.

"So you like cold pizza?" concluded Tim.

"It's the only smart way to eat it, as far as I'm concerned," said Rooster.

Mrs. Yuler called for the next question. "Roseann, what would you like to know about Rooster?"

Roseann began licking her fingers again.

"Oh, please don't do that." Mrs. Yuler shook her head. "It's so distracting."

"I can't help myself."

"Why not?"

"I'm nervous. Like he is."

"But he's not licking his fingers."

"No. Goddamn hill. Heh, heh. That's a funny one."

"Roseann, I thought we said no more of that kind of talk."

"He started it."

"No more, Roseann."

"I'm sorry."

"Now get on with your question. What would you like to know about Rooster?"

"I won't say it again. I'm sorry."

"What's your question, Roseann?"

"Uhm." She removed her glasses and rubbed them with the fingers that had just been in her mouth. "Uhm." She put her glasses back on. "Tell me what you know about bowling."

Rooster smiled to himself. This was a question he'd been hoping for.

"It's funny you should ask me that, Roseann," he said.

"It is?"

"Yes, it is."

"How come it's so funny?"

"Because I don't know anything about bowling." He had to remind himself not to look happy as he said it.

"You don't?"

"Nothing."

"You've never bowled before?"

"Once. At a birthday party. I dropped a ten-pin ball on my toe and I cried for three hours."

"Three hours?"

"Uh-huh."

"You cried for three goddamn hours?"

"Roseann. One more time and you're out," said Mrs. Yuler.

"I'm sorry. I won't say it again."

"My toe was the size of a smokie. It was all black and

blue. One of the worst days of my life and it happened at a bowling alley."

"Were your mother and father with you?" said Dorothy-Jane-Anne. She had a very compassionate way of talking. Her voice was much softer and gentler than Roseann's.

"Yes, they were, actually."

"Didn't they help you?"

"Yes, they did. My dad picked me up. Mom bought me a pop, I think."

"They couldn't stop you from crying?"

"Apparently not. I cried for a long time."

"How old were you?"

"I think I was about five. Maybe six."

"Why did they let such a little boy pick up such a big ball?"

"I wandered away to a different lane. They didn't see me until it was too late."

"Weren't they watching you?"

"I was pretty sneaky."

"Were they drinking?"

"Okay, Dorothy-Jane-Anne," said Mrs. Yuler. "That's enough. Rooster answered the question."

"No he never."

"Yes, he did. Let's move on, please."

Rooster smiled in relief. Truthfully, he had bowled several times in his life and had enjoyed himself each time, including many fun outings at birthday parties when he was still in elementary school. It was only a couple of months ago that he had dropped a ball on his foot, during a night out with Jolene, Jayson and Puffs. It had hurt his big toe, but it hadn't made him cry.

"Percival? You've been unusually quiet so far," said Mrs. Yuler. "What would you like to ask Rooster?"

Percival was a towering man with messy gray hair and a brooding face. He shook his head glumly from side to side in response to Mrs. Yuler. Then he turned away from her to look out the window.

"Oh, come on now. What's the matter? You always have something to say." Mrs. Yuler prodded him for a question.

Percival remained silent. Then, finally, he faced her again and exploded. "The man's a moron!" he said, slamming his hand on the table. His voice hissed out of his mouth like air from a high-pressure hose. "He drops bowling balls on his toes! He gets lost with his parents! I can't work with someone like him! Throw him out!"

Mrs. Yuler was used to these outbursts from Percival, as were the other members of the Strikers. "No name-calling, Percival," she said. "That's a house rule and it will not be broken."

"I can't help myself! I've sat here too long without saying anything! Now it's coming out of my ears!"

From his chair, Rooster stared at Percival with a mixture of fear and horror.

"He doesn't even like bowling! How can we work with someone who doesn't even like bowling?!"

"He got me into trouble," said Roseann. She was waving her wet fingers in front of her face. "Goddamn hill. Heh, heh."

"Roseann," said Mrs. Yuler, "did you just say what I think you just said?"

"I'm sorry. I won't say it again. I'm sorry."

"That's the absolute last time."

"He started it."

"Roseann."

"Do you like it when Percival calls you a moron?" said Dorothy-Jane-Anne.

Rooster looked at her in surprise. "Do I *like* it?"

"Uh-huh."

"No. Why, am I supposed to like it?"

"How come you didn't say anything?"

Rooster had no immediate answer to that question. Under any other circumstances, he would have retaliated for the remark, either with a choice selection of name-calling or with his fists. But he was way out of his element now. He was no longer thinking of ways to blow the interview. He just wanted to survive it.

"I guess it didn't bother me," he said in reply to Dorothy-Jane-Anne. "I don't know."

"It didn't bother you that he called you a moron?"

"I don't know. I don't know why I didn't say anything."

"Have you been called a moron lots before?"

"I wouldn't say lots."

"A few times?"

"Probably, yes. A few times."

"Did you ever say anything?"

"I probably did, yes."

"Why not this time?"

Rooster shook his head. He was on the brink of an eruption himself when Tim piped up and interrupted him.

"I've decided that I like cold pizza too," Tim said. He was rocking in his chair, and his eyes were as big and lively as a squirrel's. "I think, I think Rooster has a really good point there. It's a really good point, and after thinking about it long and hard, I've decided that I agree with him. There's nothing wrong with cold pizza. It doesn't burn you. It's easier to eat. And it's a good way to make the pizza last longer. That's one that he didn't think of. So I'm with you on that one, buddy. I'm with you. Rock on." He raised his fist in the air and shook it toward Rooster. "I'm with you on that one."

Rooster stared at Tim for a moment and didn't respond.

"Rock 'n' roll," said Tim, beaming with the decision he'd made.

"I really need a cigarette," Rooster said finally, to no one in particular. "I need air." He rose to leave.

"Maybe we could all take a break," said Mrs. Yuler, glancing at her watch. "Five minutes? Is that enough?"

"I'll let you know," said Rooster. He slipped past her and quickly walked out of the office and toward the front doors. Mrs. Nixon went after him. She caught up with him outside near the front courtyard, where a few of the other Common House residents were enjoying the late sun on a warm spring day.

"I'm glad to see you're not turning this into an escape attempt," she said, coming up beside him.

He pulled long and hard on his cigarette and closed his eyes as he held the smoke in his lungs. "I cannot go back in there," he said, after exhaling.

"You have to," said Mrs. Nixon.

"No I don't."

"Yes you do."

He gulped before speaking again. "This isn't about blowing off the interview anymore, if that's what you're thinking. Those people are going to kill me in there. They're going to freakin' kill me."

"Oh, they are not."

"Oh, they are too. God almighty. Cold pizza. Calling me a moron."

"You've been called worse, I'm sure."

He shook his head. "Don't you think it's weird in there? It's like we're on some other planet. It's like these people have taken over Common House and now they want to expand. They want me to help them expand and take over all of Winston."

"What did you think they were going to be like? Were you expecting a neat little docile group of people sitting in their chairs with knitted blankets pulled over their legs, begging you to take them bowling?"

"That would have been nice."

"It would have been easy, you mean."

"Easy to what?"

"Easy to brush them off. That's what you wanted, wasn't it? No emotional connections. No memories of any kind. Just in and out, real quick."

"You think I'm emotionally connected with those people in there?"

"Do you think you're going to forget them any time soon?"

"With the help of a large amount of alcohol, I plan on forgetting them in about twenty minutes."

"Finish your cigarette and let's go see what they have to say."

He took another drag. "I'm not going in there."

Mrs. Nixon remained adamant. "Listen, if they say they don't want you as their team leader, I'll tell Mrs. Helmsley that you tried your best. It just didn't work out. If you refuse to go back, I'll have to tell her you quit. Which would you rather live with?"

"And if they say yes to having me as their team leader? An offer that I've never actually extended, by the way."

Mrs. Nixon smiled encouragingly. "I think you're up to the challenge, Rooster. I really do. I think it would be good for everyone if you took them on. You just have to spend some time getting to know them."

"Seriously?"

"Of course."

"You think I could actually take these guys bowling and change their lives, or whatever Helmsley wants me to do?"

u can, yes. I really do."

back at her. "Okay. Why?"

...y.

"Yes. I asked you before why you thought I could do this and you never came up with anything. You were saved by Helmsley barging into your office. But since we're alone now, I'd love to hear it. Why do you think I could do this? Because I sure as hell don't think I could."

Once again, just as she had the first time this question had been raised, Mrs. Nixon had to think for a moment. For the second time, no clear reasons came springing to her mind. "Oh, Rooster." She rubbed her forehead. "Rooster, let me be honest about this. When Mrs. Helmsley suggested your name for this project, I thought she'd gone crazy. I was totally dead set against it. I thought she would ruin my idea if you became a part of it. But you know, people like you. I'm not completely sure why they like you, but they do. I mean, you're funny. You're clever. You can be smart when you want to be. I thought the first time you sang 'Here Comes the Bride' was one of the sweetest things I'd ever heard. Of course, then you did it over and over and over again until I was ready to tear your hair out."

"So I should do this because people like me? That's the only thing I have going for me?"

"Not everything you need to make it in this world comes from a textbook, Rooster. After meeting the

Strikers, I'm not so sure that the girls I had chosen could have done this at all. They're both very bright and very sweet, but I don't think the people in there need bright and sweet. They need something else and I'm not even sure what it is, but I think you have it and I think you could provide it for them."

Rooster thought for another moment. "Do you think they're gonna offer it to me?"

"That I don't know."

"Do you think it's possible?"

"Well, you certainly made your first impression a lasting one. If that has any bearing on their decision, I would have to say no."

"But—"

"But who knows if it will or not. Tim seems to like you. Dorothy-Jane-Anne can't take her eyes off you. Roseann and Percival don't care for you very much. If the vote is a tie, Mrs. Yuler will have the final say. I don't know what she thinks of you."

Rooster dropped his cigarette and mashed it out with his foot. "If Roseann touches me after her fingers have been in her mouth, I'm gonna freak. I'm telling you in advance."

"I'll freak too, if she touches me," said Mrs. Nixon. "Are you ready to go see?"

He took a deep breath and closed his eyes. If Mrs. Nixon was right, and he agreed with her logic, he had a fifty-fifty chance of getting out cleanly. They weren't the greatest odds in the world, but under the circumstances, they were as good as he could hope for. "All right," he said.

They re-entered Common House and proceeded to the office. A smiling Mrs. Yuler greeted them. "Well," she said, "welcome back. We had a little meeting while you were away. Rooster, the Strikers and I would like to offer you the position of team leader."

Rooster was taken aback. *They made their decision that fast? Where was the show of hands? The final debate?*

"It was unanimous," she added.

"Unanimous?" Mrs. Nixon and Rooster spoke simultaneously. Their faces registered the same level of surprise.

"Well, Percival didn't vote," said Mrs. Yuler.

"Yes he did," said Roseann. "He did so vote."

"He did not, Roseann. We talked about this."

"Yes he did. He voted no."

"He spoiled his ballot. He slammed his hand on the table and he kept shouting 'No! No! No!' But that is not how we conduct a vote here at Common House, and after several warnings he was told he no longer had one."

"But the rest of you voted for Rooster, right?" said Mrs. Nixon, looking hopeful.

"We sure did," said Tim. "We sure did. I'm looking forward to working with him. I really am. I think it's gonna be good. I think it's gonna be real good. Really really good."

"Yes, they did," said Mrs. Yuler.

"So the majority would have won anyway," said Mrs. Nixon, turning to Rooster. "With Percival's vote or without it. Majority rules, remember? Congratulations."

"Mrs. Yuler said if we didn't take Rooster, we wouldn't get nobody," said Dorothy-Jane-Anne. "That's why we all voted yes."

Rooster had been about to shake Mrs. Nixon's outstretched hand. But he didn't. He let his own hand fall by his side and looked at Dorothy-Jane-Anne for a moment. For some reason, he was not completely surprised that such an odd meeting would end this way. And on the upside, at least he knew where he stood.

"That is true. I did say that," said Mrs. Yuler.

"Goddamn hill," said Roseann, to herself but out loud. "Heh, heh."

The meeting ended shortly after that.

6

*I*mmediately after the meeting with the Strikers, Rooster went to Puffs' house. "I need a whiskey," he said, lighting another cigarette. "No mix. No ice. No glass. Just put the bottle on the table and go back to what you were doing."

Puffs was currently living with his mom in a spacious house near the lake in north Winston, about three blocks from Common House. Mrs. Davis was out most nights. If she was not meeting with clients, caterers, hall managers, entertainers or other people related to her work, she was attending one of the many weddings, anniversary celebrations, or fundraisers that she organized.

When she was home, she threw lavish parties with guests ranging from neighbors and relatives to local and national politicians for whom she worked. This meant, among other things, that there was always a steady and broad supply of liquor in the house. Rooster, Jayson and Puffs frequently took advantage of it.

"Trouble in Cobbville?" said Puffs. He'd just finished his social studies homework and was ready for a break. He'd also written up two more invoices for computer jobs he'd recently completed, meaning more money would soon be coming his way. In other words, his spirits were as high as Rooster's were low.

Rooster slumped into a kitchen chair and let his head fall back. For a moment he said nothing. Then he turned to Puffs and repeated his request. "Whiskey?" he said.

"Thursday?" said Puffs. "I thought we were gonna lay off the weeknight assaults on my mom's supply until school was out."

"I don't remember anything about that."

Puffs hesitated. "Maybe that was something Jayson and I talked about."

"It certainly wasn't with me. And with the kind of day I'm having, it wouldn't matter anyway."

Puffs pulled out a chair and sat down. "Why? What happened?"

Rooster had not intended to spill the contents of his day until he had a drink in his hand, but he did anyway, beginning with his meeting in the morning with Mrs. Nixon. When he finished, Puffs sat and stared at him in silence.

"Bowling?" he finally said. It was all he could come up with for an initial comment.

Rooster nodded glumly.

"You're taking four people from Common House to the Winston Bowling alley?"

Rooster continued to nod.

"For the next six weeks?"

"Until school's out."

"And none of them like you?"

"One does. A really spunky little guy who wants to be a rock star."

"What are the women like?"

"They're weird. One of them sticks her whole hand in her mouth and sucks on her fingers."

"What's so weird about that?"

"Then she cleans her glasses with them. It's like, 'Could you be more disgusting if you tried?'"

"What about the other one?"

"The other one did not take her eyes off me the whole time I was there. I sat in that chair for an hour and she did not take her eyes off me once."

"Wouldn't that mean she likes you?"

"No. She's just weird. She's like the other one, except she doesn't suck on her fingers. She asks me questions all the time. One after another after another after another. 'Do you like being called a moron? How come you didn't say nothing after he called you a moron? Are you a moron?' And she was staring at me the whole time. I'm gonna have nightmares of her staring at me."

"One of them called you a moron, I take it?"

"Percival, this guy who's about fourteen feet tall. He talks like he's being strangled, which gives me a good idea, now that I think about it. Halfway through the interview he slams his hand down on the table, calls me a moron and screams at the woman running the place to throw me out."

"What did she say?"

"She says to him, 'No name-calling, Percival. It's against the rules.' Like there's rules in that place. Right. Rule number one. Don't stick both hands in your mouth at one time. Suck all the fingers on your one hand, then switch. Rule number two. Don't call people morons. Number three. Repeat yourself as often as you can. You should hear this Tim guy talk. 'Okay, okay, okay. I'll ask the first question. I'll ask it. I'll ask. I'm ready. Oh boy. Rock 'n' roll. I'm ready. I'm ready.'"

Puffs got up from his chair and walked toward the telephone on the wall next to the refrigerator.

"What are you doing?" said Rooster.

"I'm getting Jayson over here. Then I'm gonna get you a drink. You've earned one tonight."

Jayson showed up at the door half an hour later. By that time, Rooster had phoned his mom and told her that he was getting help in math and social studies from Puffs and would likely be sleeping over. She was skeptical, but he eventually convinced her that he was telling the truth. She asked him how the meeting at Common House went, and he told her, for simplicity's sake, that he had decided to take the position after all, but that everything was still fine.

When Jayson arrived, Puffs, who was still in the mood for fun regardless of Rooster's situation, told him that Rooster was despondent because Jolene had just dropped him for another guy.

"They're still friends, though," Puffs added. "Don't say anything bad about her. You'll get him upset."

"They really broke up?" Jayson said, taking the bait immediately. He was vulnerable to such stories: He had been dumped by three different girls in grade eleven, prompting him to make a pledge with himself to remain single for the rest of his high school days.

"Go see for yourself," said Puffs. "He's in the kitchen. He's on his third drink already and I just got the bottle out."

Jayson went into the kitchen and slapped a big thick hand on the back of Rooster's shoulders. "Buddy," he said, "Puffs just told me about your day. The Jay-man feels your pain."

Rooster nodded in silence and took another sip of his drink, which was actually his first.

"You wanna talk about it?" Jayson sat down in the chair vacated by Puffs.

Rooster shook his head. "It's too weird. I've been through it enough already tonight. I just wanna forget about it."

Jayson nodded understandingly. "Not a problem. This guy won't say another word."

"Puffs told you everything anyway, right? Who did what and all that?"

"He did." Jayson continued to nod his big bald head. "He gave the Jay-dog the goods. Pretty incredible."

"Well, I had it coming, apparently."

"That's what she said?"

"We had a meeting this morning. She laid it all out for me."

Jayson frowned. "She called a meeting?"

"We sat and talked. She told me all the reasons she was doing it, and I just sat there thinking, 'Is this happening? Am I really here right now?'"

"What reasons did she give you?"

Rooster shrugged. "I goof around too much. I'm not serious about anything. My marks."

"Your marks?"

"Stupid, eh? You'd think she'd be used to it by now. Every year around this time I'm failing, and every year at the end of June I pass."

"Did she say anything about...the other party?" Jayson asked this tentatively, not wanting to rock the boat too much.

"Of course," said Rooster with a shrug.

"She did?"

"That's what this is all about." Rooster held up his glass and took another sip.

"Do you mind if I ask who it is?"

Rooster shook his head. "I just finished telling Puffs. I'm done for the night."

Jayson sat back in his chair and shook his head. Puffs joined them at the table with a drink. He passed Jayson a can of Coke and listened in.

"You've heard all this already?" Jayson said to Puffs.

Puffs nodded solemnly.

"This is wild, man. Jayson's never heard anything like this before." He turned back to Rooster. "Where did she get the idea to do it like this?"

"Mrs. Helmsley," said Rooster. The whiskey was starting to make him feel better. "Old Big Bird from Hell had a hand in it."

Jayson was stunned. "Mrs. Helmsley?"

"Uh-huh. They came up with a plan together. They had a plan. I had a plan. Everyone had a plan. But good ole Irving set me straight. He said, 'Rooster, for your sake, I hope your plan works. But if it doesn't, you won't be the first person in this kitchen to fail.' How's that for a confidence booster? Being compared to him."

"You told Irving about all this?" said Jayson.

"He knew anyway. She called my mom."

"She told your mom?"

Rooster nodded.

"What'd your mom say?"

"She went crazy, as expected. Told me I got what was coming to me."

"Your mom said you had this coming to you?"

"Uh-huh."

"Wow." Jayson sat back in his chair. "I never thought Jolene was up to anything like this."

Rooster

"Jolene?" said Rooster, with a frown. Given the events of the day, he had not had a chance to talk with her yet. She knew nothing about Mrs. Nixon's plan or his involvement with the Strikers. "What does she know about any of this?"

Jayson thought for a moment. "Good point."

"She's never done anything like this before in her life."

"That explains a lot, actually."

"I bet her old man'll be proud of me, though, for seeing something like this through," Rooster added. Jayson frowned when he heard this. Puffs quickly covered his mouth with his hand and pretended to cough. "I can just hear him saying, 'Rooster, a young man's path to adulthood is often as unique as the young man himself. Just keep your balls out of the gutter and you'll do just fine.'"

Puffs' eyes started to water.

Jayson's jaw dropped. He took another drink of his Coke, then reached for the whiskey bottle and poured a healthy amount into the can and swished it around. "That is one interesting family you hooked up with."

"Is it ever."

"Keep your balls out of the gutter. That's the damndest bit of advice the Jaymeister's ever heard."

"I can hear him saying it now. Or 'Remember, don't cross the line or your balls won't count.'"

Jayson took a big swig from his Coke can and shook his head. "What's with this guy and balls?"

"That's just the way he is," said Rooster. "That's how he'll respond to this. But he'll be proud of me. I know that for sure."

"He sounds sick."

"I don't know about that," said Rooster, draining his drink. "But he sure isn't funny."

The next morning, at around nine thirty, Rooster was called to Mrs. Helmsley's office. He had arrived at school late. His head ached like he'd been kicked by a horse, and his stomach was rolling like a nasty day at sea. He was desperate for peace and quiet but knew he was not going to find it anytime soon.

"Well, well," Mrs. Helmsley said as he walked in.

"Morning," he said, shielding his eyes. Behind her was an entire wall of wide-open windows, through which the glorious morning sun was shining brightly.

"What's the matter with you?"

"I have a headache."

"From what?"

"I stayed up late planning a pizza party for my new friends."

"Very funny. Have a seat. I got all the goods from Pam Yuler last night. She was not impressed with your behavior at the interview. She said you swore. You were late. You asked for at least two cigarette breaks."

"I got the job, didn't I? Isn't that what I went there for?"

"You got the job because those people are driving everyone else at Common House crazy."

"No way."

"But Mrs. Yuler's not very confident in your ability to do anything good with them. The word she used to describe you was 'underwhelming.' Do you know what that means?"

"Is that even a word?"

"It's the opposite of overwhelming. It means that rather than leaving her in awe of your abilities, you left her wondering what she'd just gotten herself into, and whether or not it's going to lead to a bigger mess than the one she's already anticipating."

"I can fix that in a second if that's her biggest problem."

"You cannot," said Mrs. Helmsley, pointing a rigid finger at him. "And you will not. You have less say on this project than anyone."

"Yeah, why is that anyway?"

Mrs. Helmsley ignored the question. "I've arranged to give you some support. She'll be here any minute."

"Support?"

"Yes. Someone to help you get started and lead you along until you figure out what you're supposed to be doing."

"I don't need support. Last night Mrs. Nixon told me I'm the only one in the school who could do the job."

"She did, did she?"

"Yes, she did. And she was serious."

"Well, that's not the impression you left with Mrs. Yuler."

"So Mrs. Nixon's out and Mrs. Yuler's in?"

"Mrs. Yuler asked if there was someone available who could help you. I said I'd have a look around. Lo and behold, I found someone. You are not going to be allowed to slough this off, Rooster. The proud name of our school has been attached to this project. I'm sure the local newspaper will be involved at some point."

Rooster shook his aching head. "Did you say 'She,' at least?"

"Yes. It's a she."

"Do I know her?"

"You most certainly do."

Rooster smiled. "Is she cute?"

"I've always thought so."

Rooster began to think about who it might be. Logic said Jolene would be the best choice since she was someone he obviously got along with, but she still did not know anything about the project. Was it possible that Mrs. Helmsley had called her in first thing this morning to discuss it with her?

"Is it Jolene?" he said, hopefully.

"Not on your life. I'm amazed her parents still let you go out with that girl."

"Why?"

"You're a bad influence, that's why."

"Her marks have gotten better since we started going out."

"No thanks to you. It's a credit to her they've gotten better. If she were my daughter, I'd have grabbed you by the scruff of the neck and thrown you out months ago."

"Well, that's something you'll never have to worry about."

"I beg your pardon?"

"Would you tell me who it is, please? I hate surprises."

"No. She'll be here in a minute."

Rooster slumped back in his chair and briefly covered his eyes. For a moment there he had forgotten about his headache, but it was back in full force. He thought about the throb in his head and how black and calm everything went when his eyes were shut. He thought about Andy Gilmore's bleeding nose and was glad he wasn't bleeding at least. Andy had gone through almost an entire box of Kleenex after Elma had hit him with that ball. Poor old Andy.

Rooster's heart stopped. His eyes sprang open.

"It's not Elma, is it?"

Mrs. Helmsley smiled. "As a matter of fact, it is."

"Are you joking?"

"I knew you'd be excited. And I wish I knew what was taking her so long. She probably got hung up at her newspaper committee meeting, or the teacher who runs the chess club wanted to see her for a moment. It's not that she's outside having a cigarette and failed to hear the announcement."

"Why Elma?"

"Because she has tremendous leadership and organizational skills, that's why. Those are the two attributes Mrs. Yuler was looking for most. She wants the Strikers ready to compete for a berth in the Special Olympics qualifying round at the end of the month, and she sees no chance of that happening if it's just you in charge."

"So why doesn't Elma do it all then?"

"Because Elma does not need another opportunity to prove herself. She's done enough already. She could start university tomorrow and she wouldn't miss a beat."

"Okay, so why don't you send her to university tomorrow and I'll do this on my own?"

Mrs. Helmsley took a deep breath. "University is out for the summer. And you can't be trusted on your own, remember?"

Rooster sighed quietly and rubbed his head. The door of Mrs. Helmsley's office opened. In walked Elma, wearing a black T-shirt and dark blue jeans. She looked first at him and grimaced.

"Close the door, please," said Mrs. Helmsley.

"Sorry I'm late," said Elma. "I was at first-aid training."

"I forgot all about that," said her mom. "Don't worry, we won't be long here. I want you two to set up a time and a place to get together and lay out a strategy. We can meet here again next Friday and you can tell me how it's going. I'll probably know by then anyway, but we may as well make it official. Any questions? Good. Thank you, Elma, for taking this on in spite of your heavy schedule. Rooster, I expect you to pick up the pace and be the leader with this before too long."

Sitting beside him, Elma snorted. "That'll be the day," she said.

"Get along, you two," said Mrs. Helmsley, her tone dropping to a threatening level. "I will not tolerate any reports of you two fighting or disrupting the bowling sessions. Nor will I accept anything less than what Mrs. Yuler has asked for. The Strikers are going to be an organized and respectful team of bowlers, and they are going to be ready to join the Special Olympics Bowling League by the end of this month. That's three weeks away. Is that understood?"

Elma nodded without hesitation.

Rooster waited a moment. "I guess so," he said. "There's not much choice in the matter, is there?"

"There's none," said Mrs. Helmsley.

Rooster and Elma left the office together. They agreed to meet at the bowling alley at six o'clock Monday evening, one hour before the Strikers were due to arrive.

"Be on time," said Elma, turning and walking down the hall.

Rooster turned in the opposite direction. "Don't worry, Junior," he said. "I'll be there."

He did not turn around, but he knew she was glaring at him.

7

onday evening arrived quickly. Before he knew it, Rooster was walking down the long hill that led from his house through downtown to the bowling alley.

His weekend had been relatively uneventful. He'd gone out with Jolene on Friday night and told her all about the Strikers and his new partnership with Elma.

"This could be very good for you, you know," she had said as they slowly made their way through the ravine. They were going to a movie and had plenty of time to get to the theater. "I actually think Elma's a pretty good person."

"I actually don't," said Rooster. "But I have no say in the matter, so I guess I'll get used to it."

"You have to give her a chance, that's all."

"That's what I mean. I have no say in the matter."

Later, after they had strayed off the paved trail and made out in a small clearing near the river, Jolene asked him a question. "Do you have any idea what's wrong with Jayson?"

"Does anybody?"

"He came up to me in the library today and gave me this really dirty look and then walked away."

Rooster thought for a moment. He was enjoying himself too much to get worked up over anything. He hadn't seen Jolene over the past few weekends and was savoring his time with her now. "Maybe he thought you were somebody else."

"Like who?"

"I don't know. A rugby player from St. Mary's? The starting center on the St. Joseph High School basketball team?"

Jolene gave him an elbow in the ribs. "Don't be a jerk. He upset me. I thought he was coming over to study with me or say something nice."

"Was he wearing his sunglasses?"

"No."

"Could you see the tattoo on his arm?"

"He was wearing a shirt."

"How do you know it was him then? Maybe it was someone else who just looked like him."

Jolene gave him another elbow and then tried to kick him before he led her off the path again.

Jayson's name came up again on Saturday night when Rooster returned to Puffs' house. Jolene was out with her family, and Jayson was at a rugby tournament in Calgary, so it was just the two of them.

"Hey, do you know what's up with Jayson?" Rooster said, flopping in a comfortable chair in the living room.

"Does anybody?" said Puffs, who was amazed that his joke had lasted this long.

"Jolene said he gave her a dirty look in the library yesterday."

"Jayson did?"

"Yeah."

"Our Jayson?"

"Yes."

"The Jay-dog?"

"Shut up. Do you know what it's about?"

"Not a clue," said Puffs. "But I can tell you something that happened to me at the library yesterday." He was grateful for the diversion.

Rooster immediately settled in for another episode of what he referred to as Puffs' Never-Ending Adventure Stories. They were usually tied in some way to his pursuit of Gracie Armstrong.

"I went in there to do some math during my spare," Puffs began, "and Gracie was sitting by herself at one of the tables. I smiled and said hi to her. No problem. She smiled and said hi back. Then she took off her jacket, that little white one she always wears? She had on this tight pink T-shirt underneath. Stunning. I kid you not.

Absolutely stunning. I guarantee if you had seen her, you'd have done the exact same thing that I did."

"Which was?"

"Nothing."

"Nothing?"

"Absolutely nothing. I didn't say anything to her. I didn't even go over there."

"But you kept staring at her until she got Mr. Finkle to ask you to leave."

Puffs blushed. "It wasn't even that. It's just that every time I looked at her, she looked at me. I mean, I could have said the same thing she did: 'Mr. Finkle, can you ask Gracie to stop staring at me all the time?'"

"But you wouldn't do that because that would be a dream come true for you," said Rooster.

"Exactly."

"So did she ask Mr. Finkle to ask you to leave?"

"No. She asked him if she could use the phone."

"Then what?"

"About fifteen minutes later, Nick showed up."

"Uh-oh."

"He came in just when I was leaving the bathroom. I ducked behind the magazines. I could see Gracie and him looking all over the place for me. Then she showed him where my books were."

"And?"

"Now he has my books. Math. Social Studies. Biology. The love letter I was writing to her."

Rooster's eyes nearly popped out of his head.

"I'm kidding about the letter," said Puffs.

"Thank God for that."

"I put it in my pocket before I went to the bathroom."

Rooster shook his head. "So now all you have to do is ask Nick for your books back."

"I guess so," said Puffs.

"That shouldn't be too hard."

"Not at all."

"You two get along so well."

"We have a lot in common, that's for sure."

Rooster stared at Puffs for a moment. Then he had to laugh. For a minute he felt like the second unluckiest kid in Winston instead of the first.

He slowed his pace to the bowling alley so he could finish his smoke. When he arrived at the entrance, he checked the clock on the wall above the front counter. It was six o'clock on the button.

Elma was sitting at a table in the small lounge across from the bowling lanes. She had a binder spread open in front of her. She was writing something on a piece of paper. He walked over to meet her.

"You're late," she said, without looking up.

Rooster pulled out a chair and sat down. "I'm not late. I'm right on time."

"In my house, if you're not early, you're late, and you're obviously not early because you're just getting here."

Rooster rolled his eyes. "That sounds like another reason never to go to your house."

"Very funny. I'll tear up the invitation when I get home." She finished writing and gave him a blank stare. "Did you bring your binder at least?"

"My what?"

She lifted up one half of her binder and let it drop back down to the table. "Hello? Your binder? From the leadership class you're taking?"

Rooster stared back at her. "Was I supposed to bring that?"

"Duh, yes?"

"Nobody told me I was supposed to bring that."

"You're in high school. You're supposed to be able to figure those things out on your own."

"But for what? This is a bowling alley."

"This is an assignment for school. Straight out of the leadership class you're in. Don't you remember the hero cycle? We've only been studying it for the past month."

"The what?"

"The hero cycle." She drew a quick circle on the back of the paper she was writing on. "First you get the call. That goes at the top. Then, as you follow it around, you pass through all of these different stages. Resistance. Conflict. Trials. Change. Then there's some big final challenge that you'll have to either overcome and become a true leader or quit and be a zero. We've been talking about it forever."

Rooster stared at her in silence. "I think I have the wrong Elma," he finally said. "The one I was supposed to meet here was going to help me with a bunch of people who wanna go bowling."

"No. See, that's the idiot's way of looking at this. That's the simple way. 'I've been asked to take a bunch of very low-functioning people to the bowling alley and make sure they don't kill themselves. If all goes well, they may even try out for the Special Olympics.' The other way of seeing it is, 'I've been *called* to lead this group of very *special* individuals to a higher ground than they've ever been on before. I'm going to make them respect each other and to bowl as a team who support each other so they can reach their goal of qualifying for the Special Olympics. That is the mission I have been given, and I am going to do all that I can to fulfill it.' Do you see the difference?"

"No," said Rooster. "They sound exactly the same to me."

Elma shook her head. "I'm not surprised to hear that."

"Except that the first one makes more sense."

"I'm not surprised to hear that either."

"It just seems a bit more real. More believable."

"Of course it does. You're an idiot. The first one would naturally make more sense to you."

"I'm not an idiot."

"You act like one. You talk like one. You look like one. That makes you one. What else can I say?" She closed her binder. "But all right. I've tried my way. Let's try yours. How are we going to do this? What's the next step? What's the big plan?" She stared at him with glowing green eyes through her big, dark-rimmed glasses. "Come on. Roll out the blueprints so I can see how you're going to pull this off."

Rooster took a moment to think. It was true, he was now realizing, that his approach to the project with the Strikers was a remarkably simple one. Actually, he didn't even have an approach, so calling it simple was an overstatement. He had nothing. He had followed up the collapse of his first plan with absolutely nothing. He had devised no strategy over the weekend to bring the Strikers together as a team. He had no idea how he was even going to attempt to make them play well together.

He did, however, remember Mr. Thorton talking about the hero cycle and all of its various components. Ironically, Rooster had been quite absorbed by that part of the leadership class, an option he had taken to get out of music and gym. When Mr. Thorton asked if anyone had any examples of heroes that they would like to share, Rooster had thought immediately of his father, a long-distance truck driver who'd been killed in a horrifying crash on the treacherous Rogers Pass in central British Columbia. With a load of ninety tons of lumber on the back of his rig, his brakes had failed as he wound down one of the many steep, winding slopes. To avoid crashing into any of the other motorists on the highway that day, among them a busload of seniors on a sightseeing tour, he had tried to maneuver the truck along the shoulder until he could somehow bring it to a stop. Instead, and in spite of his best efforts, he had crashed through the guard rail and plunged to his death. No one else had been injured.

Rooster recalled the debilitating grief he had felt and his mother's endless sobbing at the funeral.

"Don't tell me you don't have a plan," said Elma, mockingly. "Don't tell me you just expected me to do all the work while you took a fifteen-minute smoke break every fifteen minutes and talked with your little friends on the telephone."

Rooster knew he needed to come up with something quickly.

"I bet you've told Puffs and Jayson all about the Strikers, haven't you?"

With the mention of Jayson's name, she gave him an idea.

"I'm sure you guys probably talked about them all weekend."

Subtley he slipped into action. "I really don't know what he sees in you, you know that?" He shook his head and stared into her eyes as if he was a scientist studying something rare and unusual.

Elma stopped talking and frowned. "What?"

"I don't know what he sees in you."

"What are you talking about?"

Rooster stared for another few seconds, then sat back and changed the subject. "Nothing. I just got carried away with something else. Not important. Where were we again?"

"What does who see in me?"

"Nothing. Forget about it."

"What does who see in me?" she said again.

"I can't say."

"Rooster."

He tried to look apologetic. "Hey, look, I'm sorry. I shouldn't have said anything. I didn't even know I was saying it out loud. Forget it. You'll find out soon enough anyway. Let's get back to what we're supposed to be doing. Can I borrow some paper and I'll write down what I think we have to do to get the Strikers working together? I do have a plan. It's just not written down yet."

Elma moved her binder to the far end of the table. "Tell me who you're talking about."

"I told you I can't."

"Tell me who you're talking about."

"I promised him I wouldn't say a word."

"You won't be able to say a word if you don't tell me. Your jaw will be wired shut. Now tell me who you're talking about."

He shook his head. "Never. Uh-uh. Mum's the word. Bob's your uncle. I'm not saying another thing."

Elma's eyes narrowed. "Do you remember what Andy Gilmore's nose looked like after I hit him with that ball?"

"Of course I do. I was right there."

"That's what your nose is going to look like *after* surgery when I get finished with your face if you don't tell me who you're talking about."

Rooster frowned. "You're a bully, you know that?"

"You better believe I am."

"Your own mother is trying to turn Winston High into a violence-free school while her very own daughter is engaging in tactics that—"

"Rooster, shut your mouth and tell me who you're talking about."

"Is that physically possible?"

"I don't care if it is or not. Now tell me."

He took another deep, resigned breath and let it out slowly. "I told him I wouldn't say anything."

"You already have."

"I haven't said his name."

"I won't tell. I promise."

"Sorry."

"Do you want to pass this year or fail?"

He hesitated. "Are you sure you won't say anything?"

"Of course I'm sure. You're the idiot, not me."

"Can I just say one more thing before I tell you who it is?"

"Hurry up. It's almost seven."

"I really do not see what he sees in you."

"You've said that already."

"I just wanted to stress that point." He was starting to wonder if he should go through with it or not.

"All right. So it's obviously not you. What a surprise.

The heartbreak is overwhelming. Now tell me who it is."

Rooster stopped again to reconsider.

"It's Jayson." He felt a pang in his heart as he said it. It would take several more dirty looks to Jolene to even the score after this one.

Elma immediately blushed. "Jayson?" The excitement in her eyes made Rooster look away and stare at the table. "Really?"

"That's what he said." He could barely speak, his mouth was suddenly so dry.

"What? I didn't hear that."

"That's what he said," he repeated.

"Omigod," said Elma, putting her hand to her chest. "Be still my beating heart. Jayson Cullen likes me."

"He may have been joking. I don't know."

Elma got serious again. "Make up your mind. He either likes me or he doesn't."

"Well, he said he did." Rooster didn't know where to go with it anymore.

"Then he does. He likes me. Period."

"But like I said, I don't see how."

"Is that really for you to know?"

"Probably not."

"Did he send you here today to validate his feelings for me?"

"No. He doesn't even know I'm here."

"Would you like it if your best friend asked you why you liked Jolene?"

"It's obvious why I like Jolene."

"Okay. Would you like it if her best friend asked her why she likes you? Because that isn't obvious either."

"Probably not."

"All right then. Leave it alone. Let the man think for himself." Elma pulled her binder back toward her. "Thank you for telling me."

"You're welcome." Not surprisingly, Rooster did not feel as relieved as he had hoped, but at least she wasn't leaving.

"You're a weasel for saying anything, by the way. I would kill my best friend if she ever did anything like that."

"You just said thank you."

"I know. But if you were my best friend, I'd kill you for doing what you just did. You've violated the sacred trust of friendship. He told you something in confidence, and you blabbed it to the one person he least wanted to know."

"I did it for you."

"Bull. You did it so I would shut up about your nonexistent plan."

"I did not." He tried his best to sound indignant.

"Okay, where is it?"

"I told you, it's not written down."

"You have a plan that's not written down?"

"Yes."

"That's called an idea. An idea is different than a plan. A plan is something that's mapped out. It has a beginning and a middle and an end. Things actually happen in it. An idea is just some cloudy little picture floating around in your brain, and in your case it doesn't have much room to float in."

"You're funny, you know that?" said Rooster. He was floundering now. He had no ground to stand on. He'd created a lie about one of his best friends, and it had gotten him nowhere. He was about to begin a project that could make or break his final year of high school, and he had no clue how to proceed with it.

"Maybe that's one of the things Jayson likes about me," said Elma, who looked like she might be enjoying the best night of her life.

Rooster stared at her. He was about to tell her the truth and wipe that smug little grin off her face when he heard a familiar voice call out from the front entrance, "There he is, goddamn it." It was Roseann. The Strikers had arrived.

8

*H*alfway through the first game, Percival went crazy after he picked up a ball Roseann had touched with her wet fingers.

"I could get sick!" he shrieked. "Who knows where her fingers have been!"

"In my mouth," said Roseann, who was unmoved by Percival's hysterics.

"I can't bowl like this!" He stomped off toward the washroom, holding his hand in the air as if it was gushing blood.

Back at the scorer's table, Roseann took a seat beside Tim. "What's the matter with you?" she said, sucking her fingers again. Standing next to them, Dorothy-Jane-Anne prepared to throw the first ball of her next turn.

"I'm not sure," said Tim. He was hunched over the score sheet, covering it like someone trying to light a fire in the rain. He was trying to calculate the adjustments Roseann had made to her score. "I don't think your scores add up."

Roseann leaned closer to hear him over the clatter and noise around them. "Huh?" she said.

"I don't think your scores add up."

She leaned closer. "What?"

"I don't think your scores add up."

She frowned. "Who are you talking about?"

"Who am I talking about? I'm talking about you. I don't think your scores add up."

She took her fingers fully out of her mouth and wiped them on her shirt. "What do you mean, my scores don't add up? They do so add up. I did them myself."

"I don't know if they do or not," said Tim. "That's what I'm trying to figure out."

"Are you calling me a cheater?"

"I might have to. I'll have to see."

Behind them all, standing with his arms crossed and a slightly frightened look on his face, was Rooster. The start of the night had gone reasonably well for him: he'd helped them with their bowling shoes and gotten them settled in the proper lane. He came up with the idea of picking numbers between one and twenty to determine their order on the score card.

"Eleven," said Roseann, after thinking for some time.

"Eight," said Dorothy-Jane-Anne.

"Eleven," said Tim.

"You can't pick eleven," said Rooster. "Roseann took eleven already. You have to pick something else."

"Okay, okay. How about eight?"

"You can't take eight. Dorothy-Jane-Anne took eight."

"Oh, I see. I see. I get it now. Okay then. I can't take eleven and I can't take eight. How about...one. Can I take one?"

"You can take one. That's a good number."

"Seventeen!" shrieked Percival.

The number he had thought of was five, making the order Dorothy-Jane-Anne first, followed by Tim, Roseann and Percival.

"Yippee!" said Dorothy-Jane-Anne. "I get to go first!"

"No fair," said Roseann.

The first few rounds of bowling went smoothly. The bumper pads were in place along the gutters. Tim announced that he would take care of the scoring. In hindsight, that was probably the first decision Rooster wished he hadn't agreed with.

"You got fourteen. Then you got eleven. Then you got six. Then you got three. Then you got eight." Tim reviewed Roseann's scores with her.

"So? What's wrong with that?"

"Nothing. Nothing's wrong with it. Nothing's wrong with it at all. I just don't think it adds up to ninety-three."

"Yes."

"I don't think it does."

"It has to."

"Why does it have to?"

"It says so right there. Ninety-three."

"I know that. But I don't think that's right."

"Why would it say ninety-three if that wasn't the right answer?"

"I don't know. That's what I'm trying to figure out."

Roseann stared at him for a moment. She did not look impressed with being accused of cheating. "Who died and made you the president?"

Tim began to rock back and forth in his chair. Confrontations were not his specialty, especially with someone as intense as Roseann. "I'm not saying I am the president."

"Well, who are you then? The Queen of England? Princess Diana? Prince Charles?"

"I'm not saying I'm any of those people, especially Princess Diana. She's dead. I'm just saying I think you might be cheating."

"Who are you, Perry Mason?"

"I don't even know who that is."

"He's a lawyer on television. On the old-shows channel."

"No, I'm not him either."

Dorothy-Jane-Anne threw her third ball and turned to Tim to tell him her score.

"It's your turn," she said. "I got fourteen."

Tim stood up and handed her the scorer's pencil. He had a very flustered look on his face.

"Uh-oh," said Dorothy-Jane-Anne, who recognized the look. "Is Roseann cheating again?"

"No. I'm not," said Roseann, sounding hurt.

"I think she is," said Tim. "I think she is cheating again. She says her scores add up to ninety-three, but I don't think they do."

"Do you want me to add them?"

"Yes, I do," said Tim. "I think that would be good. She's calling me the president, but I'm not trying to be the president. I'm just trying to count, but I can't because she keeps talking to me."

"Do you know how to add?"

"No. Not really."

"Do you want me to use my calculator? My sister got it for me for my birthday."

"That would be good," said Tim. "That would be really good."

Dorothy-Jane-Anne went to her purse on the bench where their coats were and pulled out a small calculator with large buttons and a screen that clearly showed the numbers. She sat down in Tim's chair and began to slowly add Roseann's scores.

"I'm not cheating again," said Roseann.

"Shut up," said Dorothy-Jane-Anne. "I don't like it when you cheat."

"I'm not cheating."

"Yes you are. I can tell already you are."

"Can you?"

"Yes."

"How?"

"Because I have more points than you have and I only have fifty-seven."

"Oh," said Roseann, her fingers frozen in front of her mouth. "Sorry."

"It's okay." Dorothy-Jane-Anne turned the pencil around and began erasing the ninety-three.

"I'm sorry about that," said Roseann. "I won't do it again."

"Okay. I don't like it when you cheat."

"I won't do it again."

"I'll turn you over to the police the next time."

"No, don't do that."

"Okay."

Percival returned a short time later with a six-inch stack of paper towels from the washroom. He put them on the bench next to his jacket, picked one of them up and walked over and polished the bowling ball he was planning on throwing when his turn came up.

Rooster saw him do this, then watched in horror as the bowling alley manager walked up to Percival and asked him what he thought he was doing.

"What does it look like?!" screeched Percival, who towered over the manager by at least a foot.

"It looks like you're stealing paper towels from my bathroom. That's what it looks like."

"You're very bright!" said Percival. "That's exactly what I'm doing! But I have a perfectly good reason for doing it!"

"You're stealing for a good reason? I don't think so. Put them back. Every one of them. Except that one in your hand. You can keep that one. The rest, they go right back where you found them."

"Over my dead body!" said Percival, taking a stand.

Rooster arrived to intervene. He introduced himself, apologized for the paper towels and asked the manager for a little extra patience. "They're very excited to be here," he said. "They've been waiting so long for a chance to come back. They love it here."

The manager gave Rooster a once-over, then leveled with him. "Listen, kid, I know who these characters are. I know them from the last time they were here. They're trouble. They make the little kids cry. They disrupt the other bowlers. I told that lady at Common House I'd give them one chance. Out of the goodness of my heart, I'll give them one chance. If they blow it, they're gone. Now I'll say to you what I said to him. These paper towels go back into my bathroom or you guys can pack up and leave now. Done. Just like that."

"Fair enough," said Rooster.

"Never!" cried Percival.

"I'll handle it," said Rooster to the manager.

"Every one of them," said the manager. He pointed a menacing finger at Rooster, gave Percival the evil eye, then turned and left them alone. Rooster looked up at Percival, who was joined by Tim. At the scorer's table, Dorothy-Jane-Anne and Roseann both stared at him. He took this to be the first defining moment of his time with the Strikers. It was time he held little regard for, but still, he did not want it to end this quickly. He did not want to go out without even a whimper, much less a bang.

He thought mightily for something to say.

He cleared his throat. "All right," he said. They waited. The time for action was now.

"Percival, put those paper towels right back where you found them or you can walk home. Roseann, when you come to this bowling alley, you keep your fingers out of your mouth or you don't bowl. Is that understood?" It was Elma. She had joined him from the table in the lounge, where she had been observing the night's activities. "Now what's the matter with the score card? Is someone cheating? If you cheat, you don't come back. That's the rule. No exceptions. Now look how much time you've just wasted. You could have been bowling instead of standing around doing nothing. You have half an hour left. Get to it."

She turned and went back to her table. She did not even make eye contact with Rooster.

The rest of the evening went without further incident. Percival returned the paper towels. Roseann's score was revised. The Strikers finished their game, returned their shoes and boarded the Common House bus when it arrived to pick them up.

"See? That's how you do it," said Elma, packing up her books after the bus left the parking lot. "Be tough. Be firm. Establish the ground rules early and stick with them. And if you have to, be nasty."

Rooster nodded. "You're good at that."

"If you let them take over, they will. Clamp down on them. They can be just like everyone else if you discipline them enough."

"Who says they want to be like everyone else?" said Rooster.

Elma gave him a curious look. "Who doesn't?"

Rooster watched her leave, then thought about that question all the way home.

9

"You did what?" said Puffs the next day at school.

"I had to," said Rooster. They were eating their lunch in the cafeteria. "I was in a pinch."

"A pinch? You do this to one of your best friends because you're in a pinch? Couldn't you say you were in a vice at least?"

"Whatever. Elma was all over me about my lack of preparation for my big debut at the bowling alley."

"Uh-huh."

"So I had to do something to get her off my back."

"I get all that."

"So I figured what better way than to tell her that Jayson likes her."

Puffs shook his head. "See, that's the part I don't understand." He stirred his soup with his spoon. "Why would you do that to a friend?"

"It shut her up in a second, that's why. One minute she's going on and on about this stupid hero cycle. The next thing she's got little Jaysons dancing in front of her eyes and has to sit down 'cause she's feeling faint."

"I just want to know how you're going to get out of it without hurting her," said Jolene, dipping her spoon into her yogurt cup.

Rooster took another bite of his sandwich. "I'm going to ask Jayson if he can do me a favor."

Jolene and Puffs exchanged a long glance, then spoke simultaneously. "Are you kidding?"

"I have no choice. I thought about it last night after I got home. I have to ask him to come down to the bowling alley and hang out for a while. Talk to her. Laugh at something she says. I didn't say he was madly in love with her. I just said he likes her."

"And then what?" said Puffs.

"Well, then, ideally, she'll decide that she doesn't like him and dump him."

"Jayson is God in the jock world," said Jolene. "There's no way that's going to happen."

"It happened three times last year."

"Those weren't jocks. They didn't understand him."

"Nobody understands him. That's the point. Elma won't understand him. What will she think the first time he sits down and eats an entire loaf of bread while waiting for his lunch? Or he gets that tattoo of a grizzly bear he's been talking about? There's some things about him that could turn a person like Elma off."

"There's no way he's going to go down to the bowling alley," said Puffs.

"I have to ask him," said Rooster.

A few minutes later, he got his chance. Jayson walked into the cafeteria, loaded up his tray with food and joined them. The sight of Jolene and Rooster sitting together made him do a double-take. Puffs, who had forgotten that his little joke was still very much alive and flourishing, started to panic.

"Hey," said Jayson, sounding hopeful as he placed his tray on the table. He had a plate of spaghetti, a caesar salad, two roast beef sandwiches and two apples.

"Expecting company?" said Rooster, looking at all the food.

"Jayson's a big boy," said Jayson. He made eye contact with Puffs and motioned with his head toward Rooster and Jolene. Puffs briefly frowned and shook his head, indicating that nothing had changed and hoping Jayson wouldn't say anything about it.

"What's all that about?" said Jolene.

"Rooster has something he wants to ask you," said Puffs, changing the subject and avoiding Jolene's glare.

Jayson twirled an enormous bite of spaghetti onto his fork, put it in his mouth and looked at Rooster.

Rooster threw a dirty look at Puffs and cleared his throat. "All right. I wasn't going to ask you this second, but...You remember the other night at Puffs' house, all that stuff we were talking about?"

Jayson, his mouth very full, nodded his head.

"Well, the situation has changed somewhat."

Jayson's eyes widened with curiosity.

"Elma Helmsley is involved with it now."

Jayson gagged on his food and had to work very hard to keep it all in his mouth.

"And I have to ask you to do me a huge favor."

Rooster waited for a moment, but since Jayson was having more trouble with his food than anyone had ever seen before, he decided to carry on.

"I need you to come to the bowling alley sometime over the next couple of weeks and sit with Elma. You don't have to make out with her or anything like that. Just be nice to her. Act like you enjoy her company."

With an enormous intake of water, Jayson washed the food down and sat back in his chair. He took a moment to collect himself.

"Jayson needs some clarification," he said finally. "There's some things about all this he's not understanding."

"I'm not completely sure I get it all either," said Rooster. "I just need your help with this one thing. I know it's a lot to ask."

"You want the Jay-dog to pretend he's got it going for Elma Helmsley?"

"In a nutshell, yes."

"Is there another Elma Helmsley who goes to this school or is it the one we call Junior?"

"There's only one," said Rooster.

"And why do you want him to do that again?"

"To get her off my back."

"Elma's on your back?"

"She sure is."

"Why?"

"Her mom put her there."

"Her mom put her on your back?"

"Yes."

"Why did she do that?"

"She thinks I need the support."

Jayson nodded as he tried to comprehend what he was hearing. "Mrs. Helmsley thinks you need Elma's support to get you through that stuff we were talking about at Puffs' house?"

"You got it."

"And you agreed to this?"

"Not on your life."

"But Elma agreed to it?"

"Apparently."

"Why? Does she like you or something?"

"Are you kidding? She hates my guts. I have no idea why she said yes to this."

"Do you like her?"

"Have we met? What do you mean, do I like her?"

"Well, Jayson doesn't get it. He doesn't understand."

"Jayson doesn't have to understand. All Jayson has to do is hang out at the bowling alley for a couple of hours and act like he doesn't *mind* her company. That's all I'm asking him to do. *You* to do. Listen to me. I can't even talk anymore."

Jayson shook his head. He leaned over his food to dig in again, but decided against it. Clearly he was in turmoil.

"And if Jayson does this, what happens? What is it good for?"

"I can get down to the business of doing what I have to do to get my life back in order," said Rooster. "It's a bit chaotic at the moment, in case you hadn't noticed."

Jayson nodded. He calmed himself down. Then he looked hard at Jolene. He knew it was not his place to talk about the demise of Rooster and Jolene as a couple, but he couldn't help himself. "What do you have to say about all this?"

Jolene shrugged. "I said my piece. He knows how I feel about it."

"What about all this with Elma?"

"I think Elma's good for Rooster. He can learn a lot from her if he just gives her a chance."

"Uh-huh."

"Yeah. I think this is really good."

"So you think he needs her support."

"It can't hurt."

"Uh-huh." He decided to drop it before he got himself in trouble.

"By the way, I really didn't appreciate that dirty look you gave me the other day in the library."

"Yeah? Well, Jayson's a bit mixed up at the moment. He's confused about a lot of things."

"So?"

"So...." He shook his head again. He could feel his emotions beginning to bubble over. "So he's sorry. He shouldn't have done that."

"No, he shouldn't have."

"He apologizes."

"I accept."

"He won't do it again."

"Good. I enjoy the friendship we have, Jayson. I hope I haven't done anything to spoil it."

"Not at all."

"I hope not. How's your spaghetti?"

"It's delicious."

"That's the biggest tray of food I've seen since the last time we ate together," said Rooster.

Jayson nodded and leaned over his plate. It was time to bury his head and eat. He'd taken his best shot at sorting things out, but it had gotten him nowhere. In fact, he was more confused now than ever.

"So will you do that for me?" said Rooster.

Jayson considered the request one more time. "Whatever," he said. "Sure. What the hell. This is the weirdest damn thing Jayson's ever been a part of. Why not see where it goes from here?"

Rooster nearly fainted with relief. "Thanks, man. I owe you big-time."

"Don't mention it."

"Don't forget that. Anytime. Anywhere."

Jayson stuffed a heap of caesar salad into his mouth.

"That's a buddy for you," said Rooster, looking at Puffs.

"It sure is," said Puffs, feeling entirely responsible for Jayson's confused state but unsure what to do about it.

"Would you ever do something like that for me?"

"Not a chance."

"And I would never do anything like that for you," said Rooster.

"That's why we're such good friends," said Puffs. "We have these things in common."

"What about me?" said Jolene.

"You already like Elma," said Puffs.

"I mean if you had to do something else."

"Maybe," said Puffs.

"Depends," said Rooster.

Jayson finished chewing his food and piped up again. "The Man here has one more thing to ask about."

Rooster slapped Jayson on the shoulder. "What does the Man want to know?" he said. "Fire away."

"The Man wants to know why all this is taking place at the bowling alley? Since when did that become such a big part of your life?"

Rooster frowned. "Since I met the Strikers."

"The who?"

"The Strikers. The bowling team I'm working with. From Common House. With Elma. Haven't you been listening?"

Jayson looked more bewildered than ever. He considered asking more questions, then decided against it. "Whatever," he said and picked up a sandwich.

10

*R*ooster's next trip to the bowling alley came on Thursday, at which time he attempted to impose the same level of discipline on the Strikers as Elma had during her one-minute tirade Monday night.

He quickly discovered, however, that imposing discipline was not as easy as Elma had made it look.

"You know the rules, right?" he said to Roseann as she put on her bowling shoes.

"Yes," said Roseann, without looking at him.

"You remember them? The ones Elma talked about?"

"Yes." Roseann sat up and started sucking on her fingers. "I remember."

Rooster looked skeptical. "What are they?"

"I already told you."

"No you didn't."

"Didn't you hear me? You asked me if I knew them and I said yes. I know them. So there. I told you two times now."

"That's not telling me what they are."

"Elma can tell you if you forgot. She knows them."

Rooster decided it was time to get tough. "Roseann, one of the rules was if you suck on your fingers, you don't bowl."

"It was?"

"Yes, it was. And right now you're sucking on your fingers."

"I don't remember that one."

"I can see that."

"Goddamit. I don't remember that one."

"Don't swear either."

"You started it."

"No I didn't."

"Yes. You started it. You said goddamn hill before I did. You did so."

"That was a long time ago. I'm talking about tonight."

"You said it before I did. Everybody heard you. We talked about it after."

"I'm not talk—you did?"

"Yes."

"What did you say?"

"Mrs. Yuler said it wasn't nice to talk like that. She said she should have washed your mouth out with soap."

"She did not."

"Yes. She did. She said if you were her son, she'd wash your mouth out with soap."

Rooster took a moment to think about that. "Well, she's right. I shouldn't have talked like that. But still. That was then, Roseann. This is now. No more swearing."

Roseann continued to suck on her fingers. Then she took off her glasses, wiped them on her T-shirt, peered through them to see if they were clean and put them back on. "Can you say that again?" she said, sticking a finger back in her mouth.

"Say what again?"

"What you just said."

"Which part?"

"The part about this was then and that was this. I liked that."

"I said 'That was then. This is now.' I was referring to the swearing."

"I like that."

"Do you know what it means?"

"No."

"Would you like to know?"

"You're gonna tell me anyways."

"That's true. It means—"

"You're gonna tell me anyways. I don't want to hear it, but you're gonna tell me anyways."

"I'm going to tell you because I think you should know."

"I knew that. You're going to tell me anyways. I knew that from the beginning." She began to rock back and forth on the bench. Rooster watched her for a moment, then glanced over and saw Tim and Dorothy-Jane-Anne take their seats at the scorer's table. He decided that perhaps he'd have more luck establishing the ground rules with them.

"I'm going to talk to Tim and Dorothy-Jane-Anne for a second. Okay, Roseann?"

"You're going to tell them first and then tell me anyways. I knew that. I knew that from the beginning."

His head began to hurt. "Yes, you're right. I'm going to tell them first and then I'll tell you anyways."

"See? I told you."

"Just remember, don't swear and don't suck on your fingers or you won't bowl. All right?" He stood up to leave. "That's all you have to know."

"I told you," said Roseann.

"Yes, you did. You told me. You've got me all figured out."

"Goddamit," said Roseann, smiling to herself. "I told him a long time ago it was going to happen."

Rooster shook his head and walked over to Tim and Dorothy-Jane-Anne.

"I'm keeping score tonight," he said.

"You don't know how to," said Dorothy-Jane-Anne. She'd been showing Tim how to use her calculator.

"I'll figure it out," said Rooster.

Part of his newly arranged plan was to be more involved with the group in order to eliminate the opportunity for controversy. Scorekeeping had been a key issue Monday night. He figured that even Roseann would be less inclined to cheat if he was at the helm instead of Tim.

"How are you going to figure it out?" said Dorothy-Jane-Anne.

"I don't know. I'll ask somebody. How hard can it be?"

"Have you ever kept score before?"

He studied the score card in an attempt to figure it out.

"No, I haven't."

"Was your dad keeping score the time you dropped the bowling ball on your toe?"

He took a deep breath to suppress the stress that was rising up his throat. He had rarely felt that level of anxiety before.

"I can't remember." He crouched beside Tim. "So what's the deal here? Each pin is worth a certain number of points, right?"

Tim, as he was wont to do, sprang to life like a jack-in-the-box as soon as Rooster addressed him. "Uh-huh. Yup. You got it. You got it. Each pin is worth a certain number of points. When you knock those pins down, you have to figure out what the points were and what they add up to. That's all you have to do. Then you write the amount down here in really really small letters. Really small. They don't give you much room on these boxes."

"Numbers," said Rooster.

"Huh?"

"Numbers. You write really really small numbers. You said letters."

"I did?"

"Yes."

Tim looked concerned for a moment. "I don't think so. I don't think I'd make that mistake because I'm pretty good at numbers and letters. I'm pretty good at that."

"You said letters, but don't worry about it."

"I'd like to review that. I don't think I'd make that mistake."

"You'd like to review it?"

"I'd like to go back over that, I mean. I'd like to go back and take another look at that, like they do in hockey."

"We can't do that here," said Rooster.

"I know. I know. I'm just saying I'd like to. I'd like to review that."

Rooster stared at Tim and began to slowly nod his head as if to agree with him. "I see your point," he said.

"You do?"

"Oh yeah."

"That's good. I was hoping you would. I was hoping

you would because it would be good to be able to do that."

"Yes, it would."

"You think so too?"

"Absolutely." Rooster looked beside him to see what Dorothy-Jane-Anne was doing.

"That's good," said Tim. "I'm glad you said that. That's good."

"Some bowling alleys have electrical scoring," said Dorothy-Jane-Anne when she saw Rooster looking at her.

"They do?" said Rooster.

"You just bowl and the score is calculated for you. You don't have to do anything. You just sit here and watch."

"Why don't we go there?"

"It's too far. It's in the city. It's in Edmonton."

"Too bad," said Rooster. "That would have saved us a lot of trouble."

"Do you go into the city very often?" asked Dorothy-Jane-Anne.

Recognizing her tone, Rooster braced himself for questioning. "Not really."

"Does your girlfriend live there?"

"No, she lives right here in Winston. How did you know I had a girlfriend?"

Dorothy-Jane-Anne smiled. "I didn't. I just took a guess."

"That's a very good guess."

"Thank you. Is she pretty?"

"I think so."

"Does she like to kiss a lot?"

Rooster blushed. He had not been expecting one like that. "A fair bit, I guess."

"Do you like to kiss her?"

"I do, as a matter of fact."

"Does she like to go shopping?"

"Sometimes."

"Where does she like to eat when she goes shopping?"

"Depends where she is."

"At West Edmonton Mall."

"At the mall, she likes to go to the Tim Horton's on the second level by the skating rink."

Dorothy-Jane-Anne frowned. "I don't like it there."

"You don't?"

"No. I don't."

"How come?"

"Their donuts are not always fresh. I heard that on the news. They say their donuts are always fresh, but I heard they weren't. I don't eat there anymore."

"Excuse me," said Tim, redirecting Rooster's attention back to him. "If you want to talk about the score-keeping again. If you want to talk about that. See here? If Percival picks up a ball and throws it and knocks down a three pin and a two pin, you add up his score. Then if he knocks down the centre pin, you add that one too. Then if he knocks down the rest of the pins, you add all those scores together and you put them right here, in this little box here. If he knocks them all down at once, that's called a strike. If he takes two turns, that's called a spare."

Rooster remembered strikes and spares.

"Then you have to add them all up. That's where it gets complicated. That's where it starts to get, you know, complicated. But that's okay. I can help you if you want. I can stand here and help. I can give you a hand."

Tim stood up and offered Rooster his seat at the scorer's table.

"I can be right here to give you a hand if you need it."

"Do you think I'm up for it?" said Rooster, who really wasn't sure if he was or not.

"I think so. I think so. I think you can do it. Uh-huh. I think you're up for it."

"Thank you." Rooster sat down and got ready.

"Did your father carry you after you dropped the bowling ball on your toe?" said Dorothy-Jane-Anne, who had remained seated in the chair beside him.

Rooster rubbed his forehead and tried to focus on the score sheet in front of him. "As a matter of fact, he did, yes. Do you have a pencil, by the way?"

"I didn't bring one. Was your mom upset that you hurt yourself?"

"Yes, she was. She was very upset. Frantic."

"Was she mad at your dad?"

"Probably, yes." Rooster looked around. "I need a pencil." Percival was standing by the bowling balls, blowing his nose into a handkerchief. Tim had moved over and was doing arm circles by the bench where all their coats were. Roseann was still sitting and licking her fingers.

Rooster stood up and approached Percival. He was the one member of the Strikers he hadn't talked to yet.

"Hi, Percival," he said. Percival, standing with his back toward Rooster, didn't hear him.

"Hey, Percival," Rooster tried again. Percival still did not say anything. After blowing his nose, he was immersed in the process of folding his handkerchief and putting it back into his hip pocket.

"Yo, Percy," said Rooster. He put his hand lightly on Percival's shoulder. "Can you read me?"

Percival reacted to the hand on his shoulder with a jump. He whirled upon Rooster and looked at him with the wild eyes of a man gone mad.

"Hands off!" he cried. "I'll start swinging and I won't stop!"

Rooster stepped back in alarm.

"You scared me!"

"I'm sorry. I didn't realize you were busy."

"My heart rate is three times what it's supposed to be!"

"I'm sorry," said Rooster again.

"I could be dead! I could be flat on the floor! There could be men out there right now with shovels, digging

my grave!" Percival pointed toward the front entrance
as he yelped.

Rooster turned and looked in the direction his finger was pointing.

"You're a very lucky man!" cried Percival, curling one
of his hands into a fist. "You're very lucky!"

"That's debatable," muttered Rooster. "But anyway.
Once again, I'm sorry. I just came over here to wish
you good luck and to see if you have a pencil."

"A what?"

"A pencil. For keeping score? You know?" He made
a scribbling motion with his hand in the air.

"I almost died over a pencil!" Percival was beside
himself again. "I knew you were a moron all along! I
knew this wouldn't work!"

"Hey, I'm not a moron. And no name-calling or you
don't bowl."

"How can I bowl at a time like this? I fear for my
life!"

From behind him, Rooster heard the commanding
voice of Elma coming to the rescue again.

"Okay, everyone. Outside. We're going home." Her
hands were set on her hips. Her eyes burned with
intensity.

Percival's demeanor changed instantly from anger
to fear.

"Come on. Get your jacket if you have one. Let's go."

A minute later, they were standing on the sidewalk
outside the bowling alley. It was a peaceful, warm

evening. The streets of Winston were busy with cars and bicycles. Elma pulled a cell phone out of her pocket and began to dial a number. She stopped after the sixth digit.

"I'm one number away from calling for the Common House bus to come and pick you up. Now, are you going to listen to Rooster tonight, or are you going to continue acting the way you are?"

"I was listening," said Dorothy-Jane-Anne.

"Are you going to listen to Rooster tonight, or are you going to continue acting the way you are? I'll try this one more time and then I'm pushing the final number."

"I'll listen," said Dorothy-Jane-Anne.

"I was just trying to help him with the scorekeeping," said Tim. "That's all. That's all I was doing."

Elma gave him a fierce stare.

"But I can listen," Tim continued. "I can listen. I can, I can listen to what he has to say. Sure. I can do that."

Percival nodded his cooperation in silence.

Elma turned her attention to the last remaining member of the team to respond.

"Roseann?"

"Yes."

"What is your answer?"

"Yes."

"Yes what?"

"Yes I will."

"You will what?"

"I will do that."

"Roseann, tell me that you are either going to listen to Rooster or you're not. No more games."

"I will listen to Rooster," said Roseann.

"Will you?"

"Yes."

"Because you weren't before."

"I know that."

"But you will now?"

"Yes."

"You promise?"

"Yes. I promise."

Elma lowered her cell phone. "Okay. Thank you. Here's the new rule. No talking. If you talk, you sit out. If you talk again, I call for the bus. I'm going to move my things to the bench where you're bowling. Rooster's going to be there too. If we hear you say anything, you sit out. Is that understood?"

With reluctance, each of the Strikers nodded their understanding of the new rule.

"It's pretty easy," said Elma. "When you feel the urge to say something, put your hand over your mouth. Try it right now. Good. That's good, Dorothy-Jane-Anne. That's good, Roseann. Good, Tim. Percival?"

Percival finally raised his hand and put it over his mouth.

"Perfect," said Elma. "Do that whenever you feel like talking and we'll be just fine. Let's go back inside."

Rooster held the door open as they returned to the bowling alley. He did not agree with this new rule.

He did not feel it was necessary to muzzle the Strikers. He said this to Elma a few minutes later when all the jackets were off, the bowling shoes were back on and the game had begun.

"You have a better idea?" said Elma.

"I'm not saying that. I just don't think you should tell them to stop talking. Talking is one of the things they do best. It's one of the few things they can actually do."

"Uh-huh. That's true," said Elma, nodding her head. "But how does letting them talk benefit the project?"

"I don't know. Probably not at all, but—"

"Okay. So if it has nothing to do with making it better, do you think it might have something to do with making it worse? With why it isn't actually going anywhere? Why they haven't advanced as a team one *iota* since you took over?"

"This is only our second time."

"That's one way of looking at it. The other way is, by this time next week you'll be more than halfway through the sessions you have with them. In other words, Rooster, you may not have a problem with wasting your own time, their time and my time, dithering around with trying to keep Roseann's fingers out of her mouth and taking scorekeeping lessons from Tim, but I do and Mrs. Yuler does and my mom does. You're supposed to be turning them into a team, not letting them socialize. They can do that on the bus. They can do that at mealtime. They can do that before bed.

We're here to help them do something they've never done before, not what they do every day." Elma's eyes burned as she talked. "They need focus. They need to concentrate. They need to know that they're here to bowl. That has to be their center of everything when they come down here. Not you or Roseann's stupid fingers or the paper towels Percival takes out of the men's bathroom. They're here to bowl. And you're the one who's supposed to be making them aware of that, but you're not doing your job. That's why they keep getting in trouble. It's you, not them."

"I think you're wrong," said Rooster, trying to stand up to her fury.

"Oh, do you?"

"Yes. I do."

"Well that really rattles me, Rooster. That really makes me wonder if I'm on the right track or not."

"It should."

"Why?" Elma crossed her arms. "Why should anything you have to say about how these people learn make me change what I'm thinking?"

Rooster thought hard for a moment. For the first time ever in his life, he wished he knew more. He wished he had read more books, listened more intently and studied harder so he could talk as forcefully and clearly back at her as she had to him. Unfortunately, that wasn't the case.

"Because," he said. "I just don't think it's right."

"That's it?" said Elma. "Because? I should go over

there and tell them to talk away and have fun and don't worry about anything, *because*? Wow. You're a lot deeper than I thought you were."

Rooster said nothing.

Elma shook her head. "These people need more than that, Rooster. They need a lot more. They need more than just good-time, nice-guy Rooster to come along a couple of times a week to make sure they throw their balls in the right direction and get on the bus on time. And you are seriously running out of time to give them that—if you have anything more to give, that is."

When she finished, Rooster turned without speaking and went outside for a cigarette. He leaned against the wall at the side of the building and closed his eyes as he smoked. Elma's face stuck in his mind like hot, sticky gum on the sole of a shoe. He could see her gnashing white teeth and her searing eyes. Her words "It's you, not them" ran through his mind like a mantra. His hands shook slightly, and he probably would have butt-lit a second cigarette right after the first had Dorothy-Jane-Anne not walked by, looking for him.

"Hey," he said after she walked past him a second time.

She stopped and saw him. "There you are," she said. Then, quickly, she covered her mouth with her hand, then uncovered it. "Oops, I forgot. Elma said I could talk now that I'm outside."

"Did she?"

"Yes. I forgot, though."

"What are you doing here?"

"I forgot my medication."

"Oh-oh."

"I have to take it. I have a weak heart."

Rooster dropped his cigarette and rubbed it out with his foot. He was surprised that he was actually having a conversation at the moment. He had wanted desperately to be alone when he had first stepped outside. "How long have you had that?"

"Since before I was born. The doctors said they should stop the pregnancy, but my mom said she didn't want to do that."

"I bet you're happy she said that."

"I am sometimes."

"Sometimes?"

"Yes."

"Not always?"

"I never liked it when she said, 'No more potato chips. It's your bedtime.'"

In spite of his mood, Rooster smiled. "Is your mom still alive?"

"No. She died ten years ago."

"That's a long time to go without a mom."

"My dad died twelve years ago."

"That's too bad."

"My dad was fifty-eight when he died. My mom was fifty-six when she died. That's when I moved to Common House."

Rooster contemplated telling her about the death of his own father but decided against it. He was not in the right frame of mind to carry on such a conversation. "Do you like it there?"

"It's okay. My roommate's Roseann. I like her."

"What do you think of the no-talking rule at bowling?"

"They do the same thing at nighttime at Common House when we're supposed to be asleep."

"Really?"

"We have to use hand signals to talk."

"Cool. Like what?"

"One finger means yes. Two fingers mean no. Three fingers mean 'Do you want a snack?'"

"What kind of snacks do you have?"

"We have potato chips and chocolate bars under our beds. They're hidden there. No one knows about them but Roseann and me."

"How far up do you go?"

"Four fingers mean 'Turn the TV on.' Five fingers mean 'Stop I hear something. Go to bed.' That's all."

A taxi turned in to the bowling center's parking lot, drove past where the two of them were standing and pulled up to the front entrance.

"Is that for you?" said Rooster.

"Yes. You're supposed to get me into the cab and make sure the driver knows where he's going."

"Who on earth gave you those instructions?" Rooster knew the answer before he asked the question.

"Elma did," said Dorothy-Jane-Anne.

Rooster got her into the cab and double-checked with the driver. He waved to her as the taxi drove away. Then he went back inside the bowling alley.

He watched as the remaining Strikers bowled the rest of their game in silence. They moved very quickly. There was no controversy. Elma sat on the bench with her arms crossed in front of her chest and watched them. She had a very satisfied yet stern look on her face.

When they finished, she helped them tally their scores. In total, the three of them had twenty-four more points than they'd had on Monday.

"See?" said Elma when they were all outside. "You focused on bowling and look at the results. You guys were fantastic."

"Too bad you missed it," said Tim, starting to bounce on his feet. "Too bad you went outside. We were really hitting 'em tonight. We were right down the middle. Every time. Ooh boy. Every time. Right down the middle."

"I'm sorry too," said Rooster, although he wasn't sure if he really was or not. He had enjoyed his brief chat with Dorothy-Jane-Anne, and another minute inside with Elma might have killed him.

"Maybe next time," said Tim. "Maybe next time you can stay in there and, and watch the whole time. Maybe next time you can do that."

"Maybe," said Rooster.

"Oh, he will," said Elma.

Rooster saw out of the corner of his eye that she was glaring at him again. He ignored her.

He wasn't sure what he was going to do next time, but he was positive it wasn't going to be what she wanted.

11

The next morning, Rooster was called down to the office and told that his meeting with Mrs. Helmsley had been cancelled. He was elated. Then Elma walked into the office with tears streaming down her cheeks.

"What's with you?" he said, his sudden good cheer only slightly diminished.

"Didn't you hear?" said Elma between sobs.

"Hear what?"

"About Dorothy-Jane-Anne?"

"What about her?"

Elma blew her nose and took a deep breath. "You better sit down."

Rooster remained standing, but a familiar sense of dread began to creep through him, reminding him of the day seven years ago when he was called out of class and told to go home immediately, whereupon his mother told him that his father had been killed.

"What's goin' on?" he said. There was a slight degree of panic in his voice.

"She had a heart attack last night."

"She what?"

"A massive one as soon as she got back to Common House."

Rooster felt as if the inside of his body had been lit on fire.

"They rushed her to the hospital but it was too late."

His stunned eyes met Elma's.

"Are you saying she's *dead*?"

Elma nodded and began crying again.

"Dorothy-Jane-Anne is dead?" he repeated.

Elma continued nodding.

"She can't be. I was just talking to her. We just had our first real conversation."

Elma lowered herself into one of the chairs along the wall in the office and wept. "Yes she can," she said.

Rooster stared at her in silence. His head reeled. After a moment, Elma stopped crying again. She sat up straight in her chair and dabbed at her eyes and cheeks with a Kleenex.

He took one of the seats beside her.

"She had a very weak heart," said Elma, by way of an explanation. "The medication she took was helpful, but the doctor said she was a time bomb ready to go off at any moment."

"Why didn't they do anything if they knew about it?"

Elma shrugged. "They couldn't, I guess. I don't know. It doesn't really matter now anyway, does it?"

"So twenty minutes after leaving the bowling alley she was dead?"

"About that. She collapsed just when she got inside the doors. You were the last person she ever talked to. Unless she said something to the cab driver."

"Lucky her," said Rooster ruefully. He tried to remember what the last words he had said to her had been.

"She liked you," Elma continued. "She told me last night before she went outside. She said you were nice and that I shouldn't be so mean to you. But she worried because you smoked so much."

Rooster saw Dorothy-Jane-Anne very clearly in his mind. She was sitting at that little table in Common House, staring at him as he answered their interview questions. "I liked her too," he said.

Elma started to smile. "She said she disagreed with Percival about calling you a moron, but she still wanted to know why you never said anything to him. I asked her what that was all about, and she said she'd tell me later." The smile quickly left Elma's face. Her voice started to break. "That was the last thing she said to me. 'I'll tell you later.' Then she left. Now she's not here anymore."

A few minutes later, Mrs. Nixon walked into the office. She was returning from Common House.

"Is that where your mom is too?" said Rooster.

"No. She had a meeting she had to go to. She was hoping she could get out early."

Mrs. Nixon gave them an update. Predictably, everyone was very upset, Roseann in particular. "They've never had anyone die right in the facility like that," said Mrs. Nixon. "No one had been expecting that. They're as shocked as they are sad."

The funeral was held the following Monday in the Common House chapel. Rooster attended it by himself, but not before drowning his sorrows Saturday night at Puffs' house.

"She was a sweet kid," he said, sitting at the kitchen table. He was with Puffs and Jayson.

"The newspaper said she was forty-two years old," said Puffs.

Rooster thought for a moment. "That's probably about right."

"So she was hardly a kid."

"You know what I mean. They're all like kids. They'll never not be like kids because they can't think like adults. They'll never go beyond where they're at right now."

"That sucks," said Puffs.

Rooster shrugged his shoulders. "She seemed happy. She bowled. She had her friends. She had food and a place to live."

"That's all some people need," said Jayson.

"That's all she needed," said Rooster.

"That's all she had," said Puffs.

They were drinking rye. Rooster's somber thoughts about Dorothy-Jane-Anne eventually led to reflections on his own lot in life. He started to wonder aloud what would become of him as he entered adulthood. "You guys all have your own things, y'know? Computers. Sports. Jolene's gonna get a good job somewhere after university. Me? I got nothing. I got nothing to take me anywhere."

Puffs drained his drink and set his glass aside. "You sound like one of those drunks who hang out at that crappy little bar at the Winston Inn."

"No, I don't," said Rooster, staring at his glass.

"Yeah, you do," said Puffs.

"How do you know what the drunks at the bar at the old Winston Inn sound like?" said Jayson.

"Well, I don't, but listen to this guy. It's like he's teaching a course in How To Talk Like A Loser. I should put on some country music and pour a bag of stale peanuts into a little bowl. Then you can really go."

"Shut up," said Rooster.

"You shut up. Don't go talking like that about yourself. You've got lots of things you can do."

At that point Rooster remembered Elma's last tirade before Dorothy-Jane-Anne died. "No, I don't."

Puffs rolled his eyes and shook his head.

"Hey, he's been through a lot lately," said Jayson,

putting his hand on Rooster's shoulder. "Give him a break."

"Yeah, I have." Rooster finished his drink and slid his glass along the table toward Puffs. "Hit me, barkeep. And keep your opinions to yourself."

"See?" said Puffs, receiving the glass and giving up on trying to make his friend feel better. "This is something you're good at right here. You can become a professional loser in a bar. You've got the right slouch. You can talk the talk. That wrist action when you slid your glass over here was flawless. It was a thing of beauty."

"Just fill it up. Or I'll start a bar brawl right here in your kitchen."

"Another skill. Picking fights. You're awesome, man."

Rooster shook his head.

"The things they don't teach you in school." Puffs refilled Rooster's drink. "All you need now is some lonely woman to practice hitting on and you're done. You're on the fast track. Later, you can pee your pants and vomit on yourself."

Jayson gave Puffs a hard look.

"What?" said Puffs. "I tried talking sense to him, but he wasn't listening, so ... "

Jayson shook his head. "Jayson can't believe you said that."

"Said what?" Puffs missed the cue Jayson was sending.

"About women?"

"What about women?"

"Don't you think that's a bit of a touchy subject for this poor guy right now?"

Puffs suddenly realized where Jayson was going.

"Jayson doesn't know how you can handle all this stuff at once," Jayson said to Rooster.

"It ain't easy," said Rooster, feeling the full effects of the liquor.

"First Jolene, then this woman drops dead after talking to you twenty minutes before."

Rooster nodded. His head was clouded with booze and depressed thoughts. Then he stopped and looked at Jayson. He did not see Puffs, sitting across from him, waving his hands at Jayson. "What do you mean, 'First Jolene'?"

Jayson ignored Puffs. It was time to stop pretending that nothing had happened and to put everything on the table. "Just let Jayson ask you one question about that whole thing and then he'll stop." Jayson took another sip of his drink.

"What whole thing?" Rooster was suddenly much more lucid than he had been a moment before.

"How can you bear to think of her with somebody else?"

Rooster's eyes popped wide. Puffs' mouth dropped open.

"She was with you for so damn long. She's still your friend, obviously. She still sits with you and all that. That's good. But Jayson doesn't know how you can see her with other guys and live with that. *He* can't even do that. *He* thinks of her with somebody else and it just about drives him crazy."

"What are you talking about?" said Rooster.

"You know," said Jayson. "Come on. It's time for some straight talk. Jayson says it's time to clear the air."

"Are you saying you have visions of Jolene with other guys?"

Jayson nodded his head. "Ever since the other day."

"What other day?"

"The other day. What do you mean, 'What other day?' What other day can Jayson be talking about?"

"I don't know. Tuesday? Wednesday? I have no idea what Jayson is talking about. I sure am curious to find out, though."

"Who wants a pizza?" said Puffs, springing from his chair. "C'mon. Gimme a hand over here. I think Mom has one in the freezer."

Neither Jayson nor Rooster budged from their chairs.

"You can only bury it for so long before it'll come back to get you," said Jayson, shaking his head sadly. "You gotta deal with it, man. You can't pretend it didn't happen. It's not good for you. Especially now, with this other stuff going on."

Rooster looked at him and frowned. Then he looked at Puffs. "Am I asleep?" he said. "Have I, like, passed out and now I'm in the middle of a really weird dream? Because none of this is making sense to me."

Standing with his hand on the freezer door, Puffs shook his head.

"Look at you, even. What are you looking so scared about?" He returned his attention to Jayson. "And what's with you all of a sudden? 'I'm here to help you, Rooster. First off, let's talk about these visions I'm having about your girlfriend with other guys.' 'Gee, thanks, Dr. Laura. I didn't even know that was an issue until you brought it up, but now that you mention it, it is causing a bit of a problem.'"

"I don't mean with her having sex with other guys."

"Oh really?"

"Not just that."

"Well that's a relief. What else is she doing with them? Shopping for rings? Meeting their parents?"

"Maybe Jayson shouldn't have said anything," said Jayson.

"Oh, ya think?" said Rooster. "You think that may have been something you just put in a little container marked 'None of anybody's damn business' and leave alone on your shelf?"

"Jayson can see that keeping it all inside is not having a good effect on you, that's all," said Jayson.

"What are you talking about? It wasn't having an effect on me at all until you brought it up."

"Sure it was."

"No it wasn't. How could it? I didn't know about it."

"Denial is a cancer that has no cure," said Jayson.

"What?"

"You heard the big guy." Jayson finished his drink and looked over at Puffs, who was still standing by the freezer, but had not yet opened the door to check for pizza. "Open her up there, Puffy," he said, abandoning the subject. "Let's see what you got."

Puffs hesitated. In his mind, he knew that Jayson was indeed right: It was time to clear the air. It was time to tell the two of them about his innocent little joke that was now turning into a monster large enough to seriously threaten the steely bonds of their friendship. He thought about what to say and who he should apologize to first. Then the phone rang. Thinking it was likely his mom, he answered it.

It was Elma.

"Elma?" he said, his face registering his surprise. He passed the phone to Rooster. "Elma wants to talk to you."

"Hello?" said Rooster, more confused than ever.

Elma immediately began to cry. "Oh God, Rooster. I'm so glad I found you. You're the only one who understands me right now. You're the only one who can feel what I'm feeling."

Rooster took a moment to respond. Instinctively, he felt like hanging up or at least saying something sarcastic. But in truth, at this particular time, he could appreciate the true meaning of her words. He, too, was feeling the heavy burden of sadness in his heart. Even when he was talking with Jayson and Puffs, he knew it was there.

Furthermore, the Elma who had just spoken did not sound much like the Elma he knew from school or, worse, from the bowling alley.

"Are you drunk?" he said to her.

"No. I don't think so. Maybe I am. I don't know."

"Have you been drinking?"

"Yes."

"What have you had?"

"Vodka. It's my mom's favorite. They went out tonight to some school board year-end party. She asked me if I was okay to be left alone, and I said yes. I thought I was. I've been crying all weekend."

Rooster felt the lump in his throat begin to rise.

"Anyway, I need to get out and none of my friends are around and I remembered you saying that Jayson liked me, so I phoned his house to see if he was there, and his mom said he was with you, and your mom said you were at Puffs' house, so... that's how I found you."

He took a deep breath and turned to Jayson.

"Is he there?" said Elma.

"Hang on a second."

He cupped the mouthpiece with his hand. "Elma would like to spend some time with you tonight."

Jayson stared at Rooster without responding. Puffs, who had returned to his chair at the table, cupped his hands around his forehead and began to shake his head slowly back and forth.

"She's very upset about Dorothy-Jane-Anne."

Jayson, his forehead folded into a frown, continued to say nothing.

Rooster heard Elma say something over the phone.

"What's that?" he said, raising the receiver to his ear. Expecting to hear Elma's voice, he got a dial tone instead. "Huh," he said, lowering the phone. "She hung up."

At that point, Jayson spoke. "Elma wants to spend time with Jayson tonight?"

"Uh-huh," said Rooster. "Up until a second ago, anyway."

"Because she's upset about—"

"—Dorothy-Jane-Anne."

"Dorothy-Jane-Anne?"

"I think that's what that was all about."

"But she's not on the phone anymore, right?" said Jayson.

"Right."

"So she probably realized she was doing something really dumb and hung up before she embarrassed herself."

Rooster glanced at Puffs, who still had his head buried in his hands. "That could be it."

"What else could it be?"

"I don't know. Does Elma know where you live, Puffs?"

Reluctantly, and without moving his hands, Puffs nodded his head up and down.

"Get the hell outta here," said Jayson, rising to his feet. "Are you guys saying she might be coming here right now?"

Rooster shrugged his shoulders.

"If she is, Jayson's leaving."

Rooster stopped him. "Hey, you said you'd go out with her one night at the bowling alley. What's the difference between that and spending time with her here?"

"There's a big difference. This is the weekend. We've all been drinking."

"You're not saying you're afraid you might actually do something with her, are you?" said Puffs, raising his head.

"You know what kind of rumors could come out of this?" said Jayson. "She's half-cocked already. What's she gonna be like when she gets over here?"

"Could take your mind off Jolene for a while," said Rooster, sitting down.

"Shut up about that," said Jayson. "You know what Jayson was getting at."

"I don't have a clue what Jayson was getting at. Jayson was sounding pretty weird, I can tell you that. And he was hitting pretty close to home too."

"I think I can explain where he was coming from," said Puffs, preparing once again to come clean.

Rooster ignored him. "But anyway. Enough with all that. As hard as it may seem to believe, I happen to be feeling sorry for Elma right now. She knew Dorothy-Jane-Anne a lot better than I did, and I feel like absolute crap. So I can just imagine what state she's in."

Jayson finished putting his jacket on but did not move toward the front door.

"This woman was literally alive and well one minute. I was talking to her. She was bowling. She was telling me about eating potato chips and being sent to bed by her mother. Twenty minutes later, she is dead. *Dead*. So maybe, *maybe* tonight would be an even better night to be with her than next week at the bowling alley. I don't even know if next week at the bowling alley is even gonna happen."

Jayson stood still and thought for a moment. Then, with a heavy sigh, he moved back to the kitchen table. "Jayson never lets his friends or his teammates down. If you need him to do that for you tonight, he'll be there."

Rooster nodded his appreciation. "Thank you."

"But there'll be no physical contact." Jayson established the ground rules. "Jayson can sit with her. He can talk to her."

"What if she's fun?" said Puffs, tossing in a fresh new perspective.

"What if she's what?" said Rooster.

"What if she turns out to be a lot of fun to be with?"

Rooster and Jayson looked at each other.

"We'll blow up that bridge when we get to it," said Rooster, raising his new drink to his mouth. "Besides, we don't even know for sure if she's coming here or not. Maybe Jayson was right. She got embarrassed and hung up."

"Good point," said Jayson, looking hopeful.

A few minutes later, the doorbell rang. Elma stepped inside the massive foyer of Puffs' mother's home wearing blue jeans, a T-shirt, a light blue windbreaker and running shoes. She carried in her hand a half-empty bottle of vodka.

"You walked over here with that in your hand?" said Puffs, who had opened the door for her.

"No," said Elma. "I rode my bike."

She joined Rooster and Jayson in the kitchen. She put the bottle on the table, then walked over to Rooster and gave him a hug. He responded, somewhat awkwardly, in kind. When they separated, she had tears in her eyes. "I need something to take my mind off this for a while," she said, her voice cracking. She took a Kleenex out of her pocket and blew her nose. "I'm so glad I found you. Thank you so much for letting me come over."

"No problem," said Rooster.

"I'm just so overwhelmed."

"I'm feeling that way myself."

"And you guys. To just say yes to me joining you. That is so kind. It is so nice of you."

Rooster, Jayson and Puffs exchanged glances with one another. The Elma they knew had never used such language before.

"How drunk are you, Elma?" said Puffs.

She smiled. "Not very. But you should know, this is how I get when I've been drinking. I become nice. *Extremely nice.* Some people say nauseatingly nice, if that's even a word. Mary Carter had a volleyball wrap-up party two weeks ago, and I got drunk and started thanking everybody for being such valuable teammates. Gina Rosen threw a bucket of water over my head to shut me up. I said thank you to her and left."

"So you're nice when you're drunk?" said Rooster.

"I prefer to think of it as the real me with all the pressures of my life stripped away. That's what makes me nasty. But anyway, if you're about to tell me I should drink more often, I've heard it a million times already, and the answer's no, I'm not about to do that. I get drunk maybe three times a year, tops. I'd rather find different ways to relax. Not tonight though."

The evening moved on from there.

Puffs baked an extra-large pepperoni pizza he found in his mom's freezer. Rooster phoned Jolene to tell her about the most recent developments.

At around eleven, they were all sitting in the living room when Puffs decided to ask Real Elma, as they had taken to calling her, if she thought Rooster had any skills worth developing. "He was showing us earlier that he can be a very good drunk when he puts his mind to it, but we think it might be a bit early to declare that a career."

"Oh, Rooster," said Elma. "You're good at so many things. I wish I was as good as you."

Rooster closed his eyes and leaned his head back on the recliner he was sitting in. Real Elma was taking a little getting used to. "At what?" he said.

"At so many things."

"Name one."

"Okay, I will. You're good at standing your ground and being who you are even when you have a real bitch standing in your face, telling you to be someone different."

"That's not a skill."

"Sure it is."

"It's laziness. It's being stubborn. It's ignoring someone even when they're telling you the truth."

"But it's not, though. It's not the truth. It's my version of the truth. It's me expressing my frustration that you're not doing what I want you to do the way I want you to do it. It's me getting impatient. It's me being so concerned that I do what my mom wants me to do that I become this crazy person who gets angry all the time and drives nice people like you away from me."

Rooster sat up in his chair. "Are you serious?"

"Of course I'm serious. Why do you think I took this project on? Because my mom told me to. She wanted to make sure it worked. The school board's been after her for ages to get students actively involved in the community. This was her big chance."

Sitting on the couch next to Elma, Puffs interrupted their conversation. "Are you in therapy, Elma?"

"Yes, I am. How did you know?"

"You just sound like someone who's in therapy."

"How do you know what someone who's in therapy sounds like?"

"Because before my parents got divorced, we all went to see this family therapist. My mom really liked her, so she kept going to her even after there was no hope of saving the marriage. She took me with her all the time so I could learn more about relationships. That's how she explained it to me, anyway."

"So you'd sit in on your mom's therapy sessions?"

"Just sometimes. When it got really personal, the therapist would send me out to the waiting room to watch TV."

"You're in therapy?" said Jayson to Elma.

"That surprises you?"

Jayson shrugged his shoulders. "Jayson always thought you were one of the most confident people on the planet."

"No. I'm not. My therapist says I'm like a lot of other seventeen-year-olds with demanding parents."

"You're like Jayson, then," said Jayson.

"Why do you say that?"

"My old man says to me before every game I play, '*Be* the difference.' He wants me to stand out all the time. He wants people to notice me."

"But people do notice you," said Elma.

"Exactly. And it's a great feeling most of the time. I like being noticed. I like opposing coaches coming up to me after the game saying, 'Man, if we had stopped you, we'd have won that game.' But it gets tiring. God. Sometimes I just wanna be one of the guys on the team."

"But if you shave your head, cover your body with

tattoos and talk about yourself in the third person, it's hard for people not to notice you," said Elma.

Jayson nodded. "Those are my props."

"Lose your props. You might blend in better."

"I don't know if I could do that. That would make it even harder."

"You've lost one of them already."

"I know that. It's temporary though. Jayson'll be back in the morning."

"Let's get back on topic," said Puffs. "Rooster doesn't know what he's gonna do when he gets out of high school. He doesn't think he can do anything."

"I've never said that."

"You don't have to. Besides, that bar routine was too scary to ignore. That was real, man. You were depressing. We've gotta find something for you."

"You sound like you're fixing me up with a date."

Elma shifted her position on the couch so she could see Rooster better. "Let me ask you a question," she said. "Pretend I'm your therapist and you're my client."

"You're my therapist?"

"Yes."

"How do I know you're any good?"

"Trust me. That's what therapy's all about."

"What's your rate?"

"I don't have a rate."

"Where's your degree on the wall? How do I know you're really a therapist and not some vet who's trying to learn how to talk to the animals?"

"Rooster, just go along with this, all right?"

"Well, shouldn't I be on the couch at least, and you sitting on the chair?"

"First question. Have you ever tried really hard at anything in your life?"

Rooster adjusted himself where he was sitting. He had mixed feelings about taking part in Elma's game, but he sensed that there was no way he could stop her from playing it. "No."

"I thought so. So how can you even begin to think of all the things you can't do if you've never tried hard at anything?"

"I don't know."

"Do you see a problem there?"

"Yes."

"What is it?"

"Nothing's turned me on yet."

"And why is that?"

"I don't know. Because I don't like school, I guess. I don't like people telling me what to do all the time. I don't like people saying 'Be here at nine o'clock' or 'You have to have this in by Tuesday.' That stuff drives me crazy."

"So you'd like to set your own agenda?"

"I guess so."

"Do your own thing? Be your own boss?"

"Doesn't everybody?"

"No. Some people think following orders is the best thing around. It means they'll never have to think for themselves."

"Well, I guess that's not me then."

"Let me ask you something else. Have you ever kept a diary of your thoughts and feelings?"

"Yes."

"You have?"

"Ever since I was a little girl."

"Rooster. For God's sake. Writing in a little book is not feminine."

"Hey, therapists aren't supposed to curse."

"They can when they're mad."

"Can they?"

"Of course. Now, I think that's something you should do."

"Why?"

"Because I think you'd have some interesting things to say." Elma put her drink down without taking a sip. "In fact, have you ever thought of being a writer?"

Rooster's eyebrows shot up his forehead. "A what?"

"A writer. You know. Books. Magazine articles. Essays."

"Are you out of your mind?"

"Of course not. I'm your therapist. How can you say that? I think you should try it."

"I hate writing."

"You do not."

"I do so."

"Jolene's told me she's tried encouraging you before. She's told me how good you are. Besides, how do you know you hate it if you've never tried it?"

"I have tried it. I've tried it every day in school for twelve years."

"I'm not just talking about when teachers *tell* you to write. I mean on your own. In your free time. When there's five other things you *could* do, but you choose writing instead."

"She might have something there, you know," said Jayson, cutting in. "Jayson thinks you're a pretty creative guy."

"Name one time I've been creative."

"Those letters you wrote to me. From Lavender? Remember those?"

Rooster nodded. "All right. Name another one."

"I'm not saying you could actually be a writer tomorrow or anything," said Elma. "I'm just saying it might be something worth trying sometime."

"That essay you did on *Penthouse* was good," said Puffs.

"I got suspended for it. How can you say it was good?"

"My mom suspended you because pornography is not allowed in our school. She actually thought it was pretty good, though. She really did say that."

"She never said that to me. She just said, 'I'll see you in three days.'"

"My mom is not the complimentary type."

"Oh yeah. I almost forgot."

"I think that's something you should think about," said Elma.

"Me, a writer," said Rooster, shaking his head. The

thought was not quite as bizarre as he was letting on. He knew writing was something he was talented at.

"You're going to have to write a paper about the Strikers when you're finished with them. That's going to be your year-end assignment to see if you graduate or not. It's my mom's idea."

Rooster looked at her in surprise. "No one's said anything about that."

Elma smiled. "It's a surprise. Don't you love surprises? The good thing is you can be as creative with it as you want. That's what she said."

"When did she tell you all this?"

"The other day. Before everything happened."

"Do you have to do one?"

"No. Just you. It's your project."

Rooster took another sip of his drink and closed his eyes again. "Are you still my therapist?"

"No. And I'm starting to sober up, and I just mentioned my mother, which always makes me nasty. I better get home."

The funeral was attended by about fifty people. Elma sat near the front with her mom and Mrs. Yuler. Rooster took a seat in the back row and listened to Dorothy-Jane-Anne's Aunt Elizabeth deliver the eulogy. "She loved junk food, bowling and television, in that order. She always used to say to me, 'Do you like junk food more than bowling? I do. Do you like television more than bowling? Not me.'"

Afterward, he gave Tim and Roseann a hug and spoke briefly with Mrs. Yuler. She told him there would be bowling again on Thursday night. He did not get a chance to talk to Elma, but Mrs. Helmsley called to him just as he was leaving and told him to be in her office at nine o'clock the next morning. There was something she wanted to talk to him about.

12

"*E*lma is pulling herself from the project," Mrs. Helmsley said in her office the following morning. "You're on your own."

Rooster looked at her in shock.

"She said she thinks you could do a better job by yourself."

"She did?"

"I'm as surprised as you are, believe me. But she was adamant about it and she reminded me that this whole thing was for you, not her. So there you go. I'm very sorry about Dorothy-Jane-Anne, by the way. Elma said you two got along very well with each other."

"We did, I guess."

"It's never easy when someone dies so suddenly like that. I know you know that."

Rooster thought for a moment.

Mrs. Helmsley, in a rare moment of reflection, leaned back in her chair and began to talk. "I knew your father quite well, actually. I don't know if you ever knew that or not. I grew up playing with his older brother, your Uncle Jack. Michael was probably the only boy I've ever met who didn't want to hang out with his big brother. He was very independent. Not the best student, but he was gifted in other ways. He just seemed to know that he would do okay for himself."

Rooster knew this about his father, that he had not been one to follow the pack.

"My mom used to run the library here in town when it was connected to the fire hall. That's probably going back forty, fifty years now, at least. He used to slip in there to take books out all the time."

"He did?"

Mrs. Helmsley smiled. "That's how Mom got to know him. She said he must have read every Louis L'Amour book she ever had, and there were a lot of them."

"Who's Louis L'Amour?"

"He wrote westerns. Cowboys. The new frontier. That sort of stuff. Not exactly Shakespeare, but they were very popular in their day. Your dad used to take two or three out at a time, read them all and bring them back. I worked there every Saturday. He'd come in and go out without saying anything. I don't think he wanted many people to know he was there."

"I didn't know that about him."

"Ask your mother. I don't know if he continued reading them after he married or not."

"Books on tape," his mom said at supper that night. They were alone. Irving was in the city visiting a friend. "He used to listen to them in his truck."

"Only westerns?"

"Westerns and mysteries. Those were the two he enjoyed most. I don't know if he even tried anything else. He just liked a good story. Nothing fancy."

"Did he ever write anything?"

Eunice smiled. "Funny you should ask me that. I was just thinking about it the other day. He talked about writing once in a while. He used to write these lovely little poems to me all the time. Corny but lovely."

"What's a corny but lovely poem?"

"You know. 'Roses are red. Violets are blue. When I'm away, I think only of you.' That sort of thing. Some were a bit longer. Depends how lonely he was, I guess."

"Have you ever tried writing?"

"No. Never. I like to read. That's it for me. I stopped writing as soon as I got out of high school. Why do you ask?"

He shrugged. "I don't know."

"Well, there must be some reason. Seventeen years and you've never asked me if I've ever tried writing before. Or your father."

Rooster could feel himself blushing as he answered her. "Somebody just said the other night at Puffs' house that they thought I might make a good writer."

Eunice put her fork down. "I beg your pardon?"

"I said, 'Somebody said the other night at Puffs' house that they thought I might make a good writer.'"

"Are you kidding?"

"No. I didn't believe her, but…"

"Who said this? Was it Jolene?"

"Jolene wasn't there. She had to stay home and plan her grandma's birthday party. It was Elma Helmsley. The principal's daughter."

"You were out at a party with the principal's daughter?"

"I wasn't 'with her' with her. And it wasn't a party. We were at Puffs' house, just hanging around."

"I've never heard you talk about her before."

"I never have. Not in a good way, anyway."

"Did she say why she thought that?"

"Not really. She just thought I might have some interesting things to say. I don't know. She just said it, that's all. That's all I'm saying."

"Is this Elma a friend of yours?"

"Sort of. Yes. When she's drunk she's pretty nice. It's a long story. Don't even ask about it."

"Was she drunk when she said this to you?"

"Yes, but don't take that the wrong way. Being drunk is what made her able to say it. When she's sober, she's nasty. She said so herself. I know, it's really weird. But she's in therapy for it, so that's the main thing. She said all this at Puffs' house, and Puffs and Jayson actually agreed with her. Then today I found out from Mrs. Helmsley that Dad used to take books out of the library all the time, and that's what got me thinking that maybe something's in my blood, y'know? Maybe there's something there."

His mom took another moment before commenting.

Rooster put his fork down and continued talking. "After she said all this to me, I said, 'But I don't even like writing.' But she pointed out that I had just admitted a few minutes earlier, because I had, that I had never tried hard at anything in my life before, so how can I say whether I like something or not? It made a lot of sense."

"Were you drunk when she was saying all this?"

"Yes. But Puffs said after she left that drinking was something that all writers do. So that's another thing I have going for me."

"Well, I know your teachers have always commented that you're a strong writer."

"I don't even care about them. I'm talking about when school is finished. This is the first time in my life I've actually been excited about my future because it's the first time anyone has ever said I might be good at something. So even if it's not true, I don't care."

"Go on. You've heard that before."

"When?"

"Don't you remember going out with your father, talking about all the things you'd like to be when you grow up?"

"No."

"You used to play that little game down by the river, with the rocks?"

"Okay. Well, maybe I do, but dad's been dead for, what, seven years now? That's a long time ago. That's junior high and high school."

"I'm aware of how long your father's been gone."

"So maybe it just seems like no one's ever said that to me. But what's the difference? It feels like the same thing to me."

Eunice stared at her son and took in his apparent enthusiasm. She did not need any reminders of how different the past seven years of his life had been compared to the first ten. Life with his father had not been perfect—he was away for weeks at a time, and he was not always the most attentive husband when he was home—but he was a loving, caring father to his lone child.

"That's very sad, isn't it," she said. "You shouldn't have had to go so long without hearing that."

"Sad is good though, for writing. Mr. Taylor told us that in English. 'All great writers have to suffer before they can become great.' I remember we had this big boring debate about it. But now I'm thinking, 'Hey, I've suffered. I've passed a test.'"

"You don't have to sound happy about it."

"You know what I'm saying."

"I think I do."

"I might be onto something here. This could be a pretty cool thing. And I even have something to write about. Elma said I have to write a final report for this bowling project."

"You never mentioned that before."

"I didn't know about it before. She just told me about it the other night. She said her mom was going to surprise me with it."

"That doesn't sound very good."

"Well, it doesn't matter now that I know about it. Now I just have to do it. The good thing is, I can be as creative as I want, and I already have an idea." He picked up his plate and glass and took them over to the kitchen sink. Then he went into his bedroom and reappeared with his jacket and a notebook and a pen. "I'm going up to Common House," he said. "I have some holes to fill in."

"Some what?"

"I don't know anything about the people I'm working with. Where they're from. How old they are. A while ago, Mrs. Nixon said I should get to know them, but I never bothered to."

"I don't think I've ever seen you take a notebook out of this house without me telling you to."

He shrugged and slipped his shoes on at the back door. With a notebook and pen in his hand, he felt like the reporter Jolene had suggested he become. "Hey, it's a new leaf. Maybe."

He said goodbye and left.

Eunice watched him through the front window. She thought about the game he used to play with his father down by the river and wondered why she hadn't thought of it again until now.

13

At Common House, Rooster sat down with the three remaining members of the Strikers and interviewed them. "I just want to get to know you a bit better," he said, by way of an explanation. "I have to write about you later, after you become great bowlers. So I've decided to do it the way a real reporter would, by talking to you and taking notes."

"You should have done this sooner," said Roseann. They were all still very sad. Roseann's eyes were red from crying. Percival sat as if in a trance. His face was tired and worn. Tim sat hunched in his chair, his head hanging low.

"I know," said Rooster, wishing he had. "And if I had listened to a few people, I would have." He was referring mainly to Jolene, but he was also recalling comments Mr. Taylor had made in English at the start of the year. The topic had been creating realistic characters in fiction. "In real life, all of us come from somewhere," Mr. Taylor had said. "We were all born in a specific place. We all grew up with certain people around us. These are aspects of our lives that make us who we are. They make us *real*. When you create characters, you have to provide the same information in order to do the same thing." Rooster cut off his memories of the lecture at that point. He was not interested in creating fictitious characters at the moment. But he was realizing, with great clarity, that he knew nothing at all about what made the Strikers real.

"You should have done this sooner," repeated Roseann, in typical fashion. "You could have talked to Dorothy-Jane-Anne before she died."

"That's right."

"You should have done this sooner."

He remembered something. "You know what? I did talk to her before she died. Right before she died, as a matter of fact. I was the last person she talked to, unless she said something to the cab driver."

"You were?"

"Yes, I was. I didn't have a notepad with me, but we talked about the hand signals you two used when you were supposed to be asleep. She told me about her mom and dad and how she never liked it when her mom said, 'No more potato chips.'"

Roseann smiled. "I knew that about her."

"I bet you did."

"I knew that before you did."

"She told me you two were roommates."

"I knew that before you did."

"They were right down the hall from me," said Tim, a slight flicker of life returning to his eyes.

"They were? She never told me that." Rooster began jotting in his pad.

"They were right down the hall on the right-hand side. When I get up in the morning, I open the door of my room and I look down the hall toward their room because there's a big window at the end of the hall there. That's how I can see what the weather's like outside. That's how I can see that."

"Isn't there a window in your room?"

"My roommate's still sleeping. I get up early. I get up earlier than anybody here. I go to bed early and I get up early."

"You're an early bird," said Rooster, still writing.

"That's right. That's right. That's what I am. I'm an early bird. That's what they call me."

"You're a rooster," said Percival quietly, looking at Tim.

"Hey, that's right," said Rooster. "You're a rooster and I'm a rooster. I never thought of that. That's pretty quick, Percival."

Percival shrugged his shoulders. "I try my best."

"So we have two roosters here now," said Rooster. "Rooster One and Rooster Two. Or do you prefer Tim still?"

"I prefer Tim, actually," said Tim. "I prefer Tim. My dad's name was Tom and he had a brother named Tim who died in the war. He was killed in the war and that's who I was named after, my Uncle Tim."

"Did I ever tell you how I got my name?" said Rooster.

"No," said Roseann. "You didn't. You never told us that."

He put his pen down. "Well, when I was little, I used to run into my mom and dad's bedroom every morning and make a whole bunch of noise until they woke up. I'd sing or I'd jump around. So one day, my dad said, 'Roy.' That's my real name, Roy. He said, 'Roy, you're like a goddamn—' uh-oh." He stopped short of completing his story. "I shouldn't say that word again, should I?"

"It's okay," said Roseann. "You can say it. I won't tell her you said it. She knows you said it the first time, but I won't tell her you said it this time."

"Good. Thank you, Roseann. I'm sorry I've said it either time."

"It's okay," said Roseann. "Goddamit." She immediately began to lick her fingers. "I won't say it again."

Rooster started to plead with her. "Please don't get started on that again, Roseann. I won't say it again if you don't say it again."

"That's okay," said Roseann. "I won't tell her you said it the second time. She already knows about the first time. Goddamn hill. Heh, heh."

"Roseann."

"I won't say it again."

"Please?"

"I won't say it again."

"Are you sure?"

"Goddamit."

Rooster's shoulders sagged. He had actually thought he was on a roll until he told his little story. He shook his head and decided to change the subject. "You're licking your fingers, I see."

"I know that."

"That's a very interesting habit. Why do you do that, anyway?"

"I told you."

"No you didn't."

"Yes I did. I told you. I told you before."

"I don't remember hearing anything."

"I do it when I'm nervous."

"You lick your fingers when you're nervous?"

"That's what I just said."

"But why are you nervous all of a sudden?"

"I don't know."

"You weren't licking your fingers two seconds ago."

"I don't know, I said."

"What about at the bowling alley? You licked your fingers at the bowling alley, but you weren't nervous there. At least, I don't think you were."

"I don't know," said Roseann.

"She doesn't like men," said Percival. He was speaking in such a hushed tone that Rooster could barely hear him.

"She what?" Rooster said.

"She knows she's in trouble for swearing, that's one reason. The other one is she doesn't like men."

"You don't like men?" said Rooster.

"I don't know," said Roseann. She started to rock back and forth in her chair. Rooster sensed a change in her, that she was about to share something with him that she had never said before. "I don't know. My dad used to touch me all the time. He wasn't supposed to, but he used to touch me all the time. My mom said, 'Don't you do that. Don't you know that's not right?' But he used to touch me all the time."

Rooster stared at her in silence.

"My mom got really mad at him. He used to touch me all the time, and she got really mad at him. 'Don't you touch her again. Don't you know that's not right?' She got really mad at him. He did it anyways. He'd tell me to be quiet. He did it anyways. She got really mad."

"How come you know all this?" Rooster turned to Percival.

"I've heard the story before."

"She told you this?"

"Her sister was here one time. They were visiting. Roseann started to lick her fingers when her sister's husband showed up."

Rooster looked back at Roseann. "I'm sorry to hear that, Roseann."

"He shouldn't have done that, you know. He could have gone to jail."

"When did he stop?"

"He was killed. They were both killed in a car accident. My mom and my dad were both killed in a car accident. A long time ago. They were both killed a long time ago."

"And that's when you moved here?"

"I don't remember."

Rooster hesitated as a new thought came to him. A thought that made his face turn red with emotion. "So I make you nervous, Roseann? That's why you suck on your fingers?"

"I don't remember. They both died a long time ago."

"Yes, I know that. But do I make you nervous?"

"I don't remember," she said again, licking her fingers. "She told him not to do that. But he did it anyways."

"Yes, you do," said Percival, who had become somewhat of an interpreter for her. "But not as much as you used to. She's starting to get used to you now."

"Because she's telling me this?"

Percival nodded. "Uh-huh."

Rooster concluded his interviews a short time later. Percival was not in the mood for talking, and Tim had returned to his subdued state.

When he was back home in his bedroom, he read through his notes and began formulating his final report.

He phoned Mrs. Yuler the next morning from school to confirm what Roseann had told him.

"Oh yes," Mrs. Yuler said. "It's true. To the best of my knowledge, anyway. I've heard similar versions from her sister and an aunt who used to come by to visit her."

"Was he ever charged with anything?"

"I don't believe so. No one has ever said anything about that."

Since he had her on the phone, he asked about Percival and Tim.

She shared stories about both of them. "Percival is an interesting one. At one time in his life, he was a very promising graduate student at the University of Alberta. Then apparently he suffered a nervous breakdown, and shortly after that he had a terrible fall down some stairs that left him permanently brain damaged. He went from being very bright and articulate to living in a home for adults with special needs. It all happened in about six months."

"Does he remember any of it?"

"You mean when he was a grad student? I don't know if he does or not. Certainly he can sound very astute at times, but that's in comparison to the people around him."

"Does anyone ever come to visit him?"

"No. Never. Not in a long, long time. From what I understand, the cause of his nervous breakdown had something to do with the death of a family member. But I don't know for sure."

Tim's story was just the opposite of Percival's. Tim had a brother and a sister who visited him regularly. His elderly parents were still alive and came when they could. On holidays and for special events, Tim was allowed to go out and spend as much time with his family as he wanted.

"He's one of the rare ones with such solid connections," said Mrs. Yuler. "For the most part, everyone else in here is forgotten after their first year or so. They'll get visitors for a while, then nothing."

On his way home from school, Rooster went over in his mind all that he had learned about the Strikers. He didn't smoke. He didn't think once about Jolene or Puffs or Jayson or even Elma, for that matter. He thought only about Roseann, Percival and Tim and how much this dumb little bowling thing that he had given so little of his time to must mean to them. He thought of Roseann being touched by her father. He could imagine her struggling and fighting with him, but in reality he knew that the old man probably did whatever he wanted to her. He saw Percival striding across a campus with books under his arm, then shuddering or screaming at the bottom of a stairwell. He saw Tim—happy, rocking in his chair, eyes wide and alive, eating a fresh, piping hot pizza. Tim's entire life could be summarized as happy, rocking in his chair, eyes wide and alive, eating a fresh, piping hot pizza because that was all there was to his life. Plus the visits with his family.

In a way, Rooster felt more sorry for Tim than he did for the others. Roseann and Percival seemed to know that their lives weren't right. Dorothy-Jane-Anne had known that. Tim was happy with his, though. He thought he had it all.

When he arrived home, he began preparing for Thursday. First, he asked Irving if he knew anything about bowling.

"Me?" said Irving from his spot at the kitchen table by the window. He'd been reading the sports pages of the newspaper.

"Just a shot," said Rooster, kicking his shoes off by the back door. "Just wondering if you had any tips you could pass on. I don't know. Maybe you used to bowl a lot when you weren't playing baseball."

Irving closed the paper. "I don't mean the bowling. I mean, you're asking me if I know anything? As in, you're asking me to give you a hand?"

"Hey, I'm sorry if I've never done it before, all right? I've never been in a position where I've actually had to do something important before, either."

"So now this bowling project is important?"

Rooster took a seat by the table. "Yeah it is," he said.

"When you started it, you told your mother not to worry because it wouldn't take up any of your time."

Rooster raised his hands off the table, palms up. "I was wrong, all right? I was wrong about everything. About the Strikers. Elma. Me."

"You?"

"I thought I had it all figured out. I thought I knew what was going on."

"And now you don't or now you do?"

"Now I don't, but I think I do."

Irving nodded. "Incredibly enough, that makes sense to me."

Rooster stifled a small smile. "I'm not surprised."

"I was hoping it would come to this, actually," said Irving.

"You were?" Rooster frowned.

"It's a sign that you're growing up."

"How?"

"Look at you. You're a seventeen-year-old boy asking for help to make a group of mentally handicapped people better bowlers. Does that sound like something you would have done six months ago?"

Rooster shook his head.

"You better believe it's not."

"So do you know anything about bowling?"

Irving took a sip from the coffee cup next to the newspaper. "Nope," he said. He put the cup down. "But I do have a little booklet that may be of some interest to you."

"A booklet?"

Irving sat back in his chair and folded his hands on his belly. "The day I got called up to the Twins, I phoned my brother. He wasn't home. I said to his roommate, 'Where the hell is he? I gotta talk to him.' His roommate said, 'I think he's gone bowling.' I said, 'What? Peter's never thrown a bowling ball in his cotton-pickin' life. What the hell's he doin' at a bowling alley?' 'He's in love with a bowler,' his roommate said. So when I finally got hold of him, and I was finally able to tell him what was going on, he was sitting on his bed in his bedroom reading this little booklet called 'Let's Go Bowling.' He was studying the stupid thing to impress this girl he was in love with."

"Does this story have an end?" said Rooster, who frequently grew impatient with Irving's long way of saying things.

"It has a happy end for you. When Peter and this girl broke up, he gave me the booklet as a memento of the day I was called to the majors."

"So you have it, is that what you're telling me?"

"In the closet. I'll go get it for you. I'm sure it has everything you'll ever need to know about bowling."

"Why didn't he keep it?" said Rooster as Irving lifted himself off his chair.

"Peter died of an aneurysm a year later. Almost to the day. I was back in the minors by then. In one year I went from the greatest day of my life to the worst."

Rooster remained in his chair as Irving went into his bedroom to get the booklet. He looked out the same window that his mother and Irving spent many hours staring through and wondered what else he was going to learn before the project was over.

14

The booklet proved to be most helpful.

"I wish I'd had this a month ago," he said to Puffs and Jolene as they walked to the store after school Thursday. He'd brought the booklet with him so he could study it during social studies. "It tells you everything. It even shows you how to keep score."

"Has scorekeeping been a problem?" said Jolene.

"Not unless you count the times when they're actually bowling," said Rooster. "When they're on the bus or tying up their shoes, no, they don't even talk about it."

"In other words, yes?" said Jolene.

"That's another way of putting it." He went through it again after supper. In addition to the rules of score-keeping, he became familiar with such scoring terms as head pin, corner pin, foul, split, aces and chop-off. He learned bowling terminology like approach, backswing, count, dots, arrows, channel, frame. He read about the benefits of spot bowling, particularly for beginners, and reviewed several times the small chapter on How To Bowl Correctly: "First, the player should be relaxed. The correct grip, stance and follow-through should then be practiced."

He even acquired tips that he could pass on, like telling the Strikers to make sure they kept their wrists straight so the ball wouldn't twist as it left their hand, and to align themselves with the darts on the lane for sighting their target spots.

"What exactly is a target spot?" said Puffs later that night as Rooster shared what he had learned.

"I'm assuming it's a pin," said Rooster, the booklet open in his hand. "But check this out. Pretend I'm talking to them. 'Hey, guys. Remember now, approach the line with confidence. It's the only way you'll acquire poise and body balance.'"

"It says that in there?"

"It says exactly that in here. Word for word."

"That's some very impressive advice you're handing out."

"You think so?"

"For sure. I don't know if they'll be able to understand it, but if Mrs. Helmsley is standing near you, she'll fall off her feet."

"That would be interesting to see."

"What if they ask you for a demonstration?"

"I've thought about that."

"What if they say, like, 'Can you show us that bit about the body balance, please?' What are you gonna do?"

"I've already told them I blew my knee out in the World Bowling Championships in Bern, Switzerland, two years ago."

"You did?"

"No. But if they ask me for a demo, I might have to."

"How do you know Bern is in Switzerland?"

"I don't, and with my luck, one of them will be from there. But that's okay. I'm on their side now. We're all friends."

"Weren't you before?"

"I don't think so," said Rooster, after taking a moment to think about it. "It may have seemed like it, but I don't think we were."

That night, he went to the bowling alley and waited by himself for the Strikers to arrive. They came in more quietly than usual.

Mrs. Yuler was with them. "I heard Elma wasn't going to be here, and I just thought I should stay for a few minutes at least. They were upset today. They know this is their first trip down here since last week."

In honor of Dorothy-Jane-Anne, Rooster wrote her name at the top of the score sheet. It was an idea he had thought of earlier. He then marked each of the tiny squares with the symbol used for strikes.

"So she won the game?" said Roseann, who watched intently as he made the markings.

"Do you think that's a good idea?"

"Uh-huh. Yes. I do," said Roseann. "I think it's a good idea."

"You know what else I thought of?"

"No. What else?"

"You get to bowl first because you were her room-mate, and I know how much your friendship meant to her. She told me that the last night she was alive. She said one of the things she liked best about Common House was that you were her roommate."

Roseann's face was about five inches from Rooster's nose as he spoke to her. She stared at him through her smeared, dirty glasses, which he hardly noticed anymore. He thought only of the father who wouldn't keep his hands off her.

"She really said that?" said Roseann.

"Do you think I'd make that up?"

"No. I don't think that. I'm not saying that."

"Well then? It must be the truth, right?"

"Yes. I guess so."

"Well, it is the truth. That's what she said to me. That's one of the last things she ever said, how much she appreciated your friendship."

"She really said that?"

"Yes, she did."

"That's the truth?"

"That's the truth."

Roseann smiled. "I knew that before you did, you know."

"I'm sure you did. Good friends always know each other very well."

"I knew that before you did."

Tim and Percival walked over to the scorer's table to see what Roseann and Rooster were doing. Rooster showed them the score card and asked them what they thought of it.

"I think it's good," said Tim, lighting up. "I think it's really good. I think that's a really good idea. Yup. That works for me. That's okay."

Percival solemnly nodded his approval.

"I have another one for Dorothy-Jane-Anne," said Rooster. He stood up so he could address all of them together. "Tonight, instead of talking, and instead of not talking at all, like you did with Elma, we're going to use hand signals. Thumbs-up means 'Good shot.' Thumbs-down means 'Better luck next time.' Double thumbs-up means 'Awesome.' One finger means 'I have to go to the bathroom.' Two fingers mean 'I need a drink of water.' How does that sound?"

They liked it.

"You guys bowled very well when you weren't distracted with all the talking, but some form of communication between teammates is a good thing. I don't want you ignoring each other."

Tim silently gave him the thumbs-up. Roseann picked up the first ball and started the game.

As they bowled, a woman joined Mrs. Yuler and watched the Strikers. Rooster, sitting at the scorer's table, booklet in hand, learning on the fly how to actually track the scores of all three of them, did not get up to meet her. However, he did call out on occasion for Tim to keep his back straight and for Roseann to release the ball when it was a bit closer to the floor. "It rolls better," he said to her. Percival he left alone.

They repeated the same procedure the following Monday. Dorothy-Jane-Anne's name went on the top of the score sheet. Every box beside her name was filled with the strike sign. Roseann bowled next. Then Tim. Then Percival. The hand signals remained the same. Rooster quickly became competent as a scorekeeper. The advice he'd been calling out began to make more sense.

"Just look. The dart on the floor is only fifteen feet away. Those pins are sixty feet away. So it's easier to hit the dart than the pins. Line your feet up with the darts back here and aim for them when you throw the ball. It's called spot bowling. It's the way beginners learn how to bowl."

"I'm not a beginner," said Roseann. "I've bowled before."

"I know that. But I'll bet your scores will get better if you aim for the darts instead of the pins."

She aimed for the darts. Her score improved by ten points.

After the game, Rooster led them into the lounge area for a surprise.

"What is it?" said Roseann. "What are we doing here?"

"This is our last time together before Thursday's final bowling session," said Rooster, who had cleared everything with Mrs. Yuler earlier in the day. "So tonight, I thought I'd treat you all to a pizza. We can call it our wrap-up party."

"A pizza!" said Roseann.

"How did you know I liked pizza?" said Tim, who could barely contain his excitement. "I thought I had kept that a secret. I thought nobody knew that."

Rooster looked at him and raised his eyebrows.

"That's a joke," said Tim. "That's my idea of a joke. That's a little joke of mine. I get my brother all the time with that one."

Even Percival seemed impressed. "What flavor?" he asked.

"One half is pepperoni. The other half is ham and pineapple," said Rooster. "I asked Mrs. Yuler what your favorite kinds were. She said this would make everybody very happy."

The pizza arrived a few minutes later. They ate and talked about bowling.

"You know what we should get?" said Tim, between bites. "You know what we need? You know what we should have? We should have team T-shirts. Team bowling shirts with little words on them that say The Strikers."

Rooster stared at Tim in amazement. "You know, Tim, that's a fantastic idea."

"You think so?"

"I really do. I'll get right on that. I'll get on it right away so we can have our shirts for Thursday."

"You think that's a good idea?"

"I'm going to make a call on that as soon as we're done here."

"You really like that one?"

"Yes, I do. I really like that one."

"That's good."

"That's really good."

"I get a small," said Roseann. "With an 'S' on the back. On the tag. A small. I don't need anything bigger than that."

"I'll get a medium," said Tim. "Big is too big. Medium is good. A medium will fit me just fine. That's my size, a medium."

"I think I'll get you a small," said Rooster, sizing Tim up. "You're a different shape than Roseann, but I don't think you're much bigger."

"Okay. That's good. I'm good with that. That's okay."

Rooster looked at Percival. "Let me guess. Extra large."

Percival, his mouth full of ham-and-pineapple pizza, nodded.

A short time later, Rooster called for the Common House bus to come down to the bowling alley to pick them up. They were a happy group. They weren't fighting or pushing.

"Thank you for the pizza," said Percival as he stepped onto the bus.

"You're welcome," said Rooster.

He watched them leave, then hurried home. He had plenty of work to do before Thursday.

15

There was no fuss or fanfare when the Strikers were asked to join the Special Olympics Bowling League after Thursday's session. A member of the committee, Mavis Brown, the woman who had joined Mrs. Yuler the previous week, attended Thursday's session, then announced afterward that she was more than pleased to invite the Strikers to join. "You meet all the criteria for the kind of teams we associate with," she said.

That was it. Mrs. Yuler clapped her hands and said thank you very much. The Strikers themselves, looking like a true team in their new white bowling shirts, seemed satisfied, but nothing more than that. Tim was mildly disappointed to hear that pizza in the lounge would not be repeated.

"What were you expecting?" said Jolene when Rooster phoned her later that night.

"I don't know. Hugs maybe. A cake. Some cheering."

"For what? They're joining a league. If they win the league you'll probably see hugs and cake."

"Probably," he said.

"I mean, it's a very nice thing you did for them, getting them all organized and everything, but don't forget, they're still in mourning. They started out with four team members and now they only have three. I'm sure they're still upset about that."

"Uh-huh." He did not need to be reminded of Dorothy-Jane-Anne's passing. He was thinking of her more now than ever before.

"You sound a bit down yourself. Are you okay?"

"Me? I'm fine. Why wouldn't I be?"

"I don't know."

"I just have to finish writing this report and I'm done."

"Good luck with it," said Jolene.

One of the very few times he had ever taken a serious stab at writing was in grade six when his teacher told everyone in the class to pick one day out of their lives and write about it. Most of the other kids wrote about something fun—a trip to Disneyland with their grandparents, staying with their cousins at the lake, the day the new puppy came home. Rooster wrote about the day his dad was buried at the cemetery in Winston.

He said that he woke up that day feeling very sad, but it wasn't until they began to lower the coffin into the ground that he started to cry. There was something about the slow, creaky sound of the crank going round and round that got him going. He cried until the sound stopped and then he opened his eyes and saw that it was over. His dad's coffin had reached the bottom of the grave. The pastor said something and closed his Bible. People started to slowly move away. Two men in a blue pickup truck with shovels sticking out the back pulled up on the drive and quietly sat and waited. Rooster discovered then that the sound of the crank wasn't the worst sound in the world. It was the dead silence that followed it.

His teacher had given him an A. She said it was very moving without being too sentimental. Rooster had not been completely sure what "too sentimental" meant, and he did not want to ask for fear of looking stupid, so he never did find out. He kept the paper in the back of one of his dresser drawers. He hadn't looked at it in years, but as he sat down to write about his involvement with the Strikers, he felt a need to read it again. When he did, he cried for the first time since his dad's funeral.

He felt better afterward. His mom always talked about feeling better after a good cry. He supposed this was what she was talking about.

He took a few stabs at beginning his report, but as much as he felt like writing, nothing seemed to be working, so he pulled out a new scribbler from his desk and wrote on the front of it *My Empty Diary*. He sat and stared at it for a moment or two. Then he opened it up and made his first entry:

Hello. This is Elma's idea, not mine. This diary will never be shown to anyone but me. However, if anyone else does see it, and reads it, they will die a hideous death, with me working the controls.

Apparently, keeping this sort of thing is good for my development as a writer, which, also apparently, is something that I may or may not be good at. We shall see.

I have just reread my piece on the day my dad was buried. What a crappy day that was. A crappy year, actually. I have never really gotten over that, I am now realizing. I think it's time to move on. Or, as Dad used to say, "It's time to spark it and drive."

Wish me luck.

Good luck.

Thank you.

16

Mrs. Helmsley had no idea what he was talking about when he walked into her office for a meeting and dropped the essay on her desk.

"Elma said you were going to surprise me by telling me to write a report on the Strikers when it was all over. So here it is. I beat you to it. You don't have to tell me anymore."

Never one to let her guard down, Mrs. Helmsley could not help but look very confused. She picked up his paper and leafed through its four pages.

"I don't know what you're talking about," she said, her eyes glancing off the words he had written.

"I'm talking about the report you were going to get me to write. Here it is."

She looked up from his paper. "I never intended to ask you for a report on your time with the Strikers. I've received a very nice report from Mrs. Yuler about how they all miss you over there. She said she had expected them to be more excited about this bowling league next year, but when she asked them why they weren't, Roseann said it was because they weren't going to see you anymore. That, right there, tells me you did what you set out to do."

"What you set me out to do," said Rooster.

"Of course."

Rooster thought for a moment. "So, what? Elma told me I had to do something that I really didn't have to do?"

"I guess so."

"Why would she do that?"

"I don't know. Ask her."

At lunch, Jayson filled him in on what Elma's plan had been. "She just wanted to give you something to write about. See how well you did. You can't tell a person he should try writing and then just leave him hanging there. You've gotta give him something to write about."

"Says who?"

"I don't know. Says Elma, I guess."

"How do you know what Elma says?"

"I asked her out. We went to a movie Monday night."

Rooster hesitated. "You what?"

"I asked her out. We went to a movie Monday night."

"You asked Elma out on a date?"

"Uh-huh."

"She was drunk when you went, obviously."

"No. Stone-sober actually. We had a really nice time. She was Real Elma the whole time we were together."

"I don't get it."

"Neither do I."

"She said she was looking for new ways of relaxing, not weird people to hang out with."

"We like each other. She's never had a boyfriend before. She likes who she is right now."

"Does Puffs know about this?"

"He was the one who helped me get my nerve up. My track record with the ladies hasn't been so hot lately."

"Puffs helped you ask Elma Helmsley out on a date?"

"He kept saying he owed me one. I had no idea what he was talking about, but...what the hell."

"Do you know now?"

"I don't have a clue. I got his books back for him, though, from Nick? Gracie's boyfriend? I saw him in the parking lot yesterday, so I went over and told him to hand over Puffs' books or I'd shove his head up his exhaust pipe."

"Did he get them?"

"After he wet his pants he got right on it."

Rooster shook his head. "And since when did you start talking like a normal person again?"

"Elma convinced me it was time to change."

"Really."

"Oh yeah. It gets tiring after a while anyway."

"So are you gonna grow your hair out and wear long-sleeved shirts all the time now too?"

"No. The bald head and the tattoos stay."

"She said this?"

"Uh-uh. Jayson makes the call on that," said Jayson.

"Hey, you just—"

"I got tripped up." Jayson shrugged his shoulders. "It's going to take some undoing, let me tell you."

Rooster went home after school and lay down on his bed. He had final exams the next week. Mrs. Helmsley had assured him before he left her office that his performance with the Strikers would help his cause come graduation time, but he still had loads of studying to do. Jolene was locked away in her bedroom, poring over her notes. Puffs was anxious for school to end so he could make money running his computer business full-time. Jayson had several possibilities on the go.

What would Rooster do?

He leaned over to his desk and picked up the rough copy of his paper. There were cross-outs here and there, and notes written between the lines that he had added before dropping it off with Mrs. Helmsley.

He was pleased with the way it had gone. It wasn't perfect, but it was decent enough. Or better.

He'd enjoyed doing it, that was the main thing.

He rolled back onto his bed and started to read page one.

When I was a little kid, I used to go down to the Winston River with my dad and throw rocks at pieces of driftwood. My dad always turned this into a game. "What do you want to be when you grow up?" he'd say, just before I threw. "A truck driver," I'd say. If I hit the wood I was aiming at, he'd call out, "Look at that! You're a truck driver." If I missed, he'd say, "Nope, you're not a truck driver. What else do you wanna be?" Sometimes I'd say something like "A ballerina," and I'd throw the rock in the opposite direction of the wood. Whenever I did this he'd say, "You hit it. I saw you. Rooster's gonna be a ballerina now. Ha ha."

He always made me feel that as long as I took aim at something, I could do it. Then he died, and I never played the game again.

Rooster stopped reading.

What he had written was true, and it wasn't until the Strikers came along that he realized he had forgotten all that.

So now the question in his mind was, what does a seventeen-year-old kid who may have a talent for writing do after he graduates? Rooster had no idea, but he was much more excited about finding out than he had been the day Mrs. Nixon called him into her office.

10 sup wa
to the store
to score a
goal

Books by Don Trembath

Teen Fiction

The Tuesday Café
1-55143-074-6 $8.95 CDN $6.95 U.S. PB

A Fly Named Alfred
1-55143-083-5 $8.95 CDN $6.95 U.S. PB

A Beautiful Place on Yonge Street
1-55143-121-1 $7.95 CDN $6.95 U.S. PB

The Popsicle Journal
1-55143-185-8 $8.95 CDN $6.95 U.S. PB

Lefty Carmichael Has a Fit
1-55143-166-1 $8.95 CDN $6.95 U.S. PB

The Black Belt Series

Frog Face and the Three Boys
1-55143-165-3 $8.95 CDN $6.95 U.S. PB

One Missing Finger
1-55143-194-7 $8.95 CDN $6.95 U.S. PB

The Bachelors
1-55143-209-9 $8.95 CDN $6.95 U.S. PB

The Big Show
1-55143-266-8 $8.95 CDN $6.95 U.S. PB